Urban Luxe Chronicles:
The Concealed Truth

Mandi Mac

NATIONAL BESTSELLING AUTHOR

MANDI MAC

URBAN LUXE
Chronicles
THE CONCEALED TRUTH

Copyright © 2016 by Mandi Mac

.

Urban Luxe Chronicles
Written by: Mandi Mac
Edited by: Gencie McRae
Text Formatting: Fountain Pen Publishing LLC
Cover Design and Layout: Mits Art Studio

ISBN-13: 978-1-946258-04-5

ISBN-10: 1-946258-04-0
BISAC: Drama / American / Urban-African American

TABLE OF CONTENTS

The Tropics

Gliding over the crisp clouds and into the orange, pink and violet sky, Omar and Ja'Bria looked out of the window and admired nature's masterpiece. Ja'Bria sunk into the plush seat of the private jet and relaxed her mind, body and soul. She was finally able to enjoy a well-deserved vacation. "Champagne?" the flight attendant asked as she poured Ja'Bria a nice glass of Moet & Chandon. Ja'Bria stretched her legs across Omar's lap as he massaged her feet and calf muscles. Her skin was soft and his hands were strong. He wanted to make love to her right there in the middle of the jet. Ja'Bria giggled as she gazed into his eyes.

This was their first time vacationing via private jet so they didn't speak much during the flight. Instead they admired the aircraft, the friendly staff and the view. After landing at the airport, the private charter staff grabbed their luggage and escorted them through the airport. They arrived at curbside pick-up with meet and greet courtesy of the hotel and resort.

Upon arrival at the hotel, they were given a complimentary upgrade to a club level ocean front room. "It's so beautiful!" Ja'Bria said as she slid the curtains opened to the panoramic view of the ocean.

The balcony wrapped around half of the hotel room, the linen, curtains and carpet were snow white. It was everything they had dreamed of and more. Omar smiled, slipped into the bathroom and pulled a little black velvet box out of his pocket. He opened it and admired the 14k white gold Three Stone VVS diamond engagement ring that glistened as the lights hit it. He became anxious and shoved it back into his pocket. He hadn't decided when or where he was going to propose, but he knew it would be on their vacation. It had been three years since the two began dating; they were a match made in heaven so it was time for them to move into the next step of their relationship. "Babe, what are you doing in there? I have to pee" Ja'Bria giggled as she pushed the door open. "About to take a shower girl!" he chuckled as he casually slid his pants off and threw his shirt over them to hide any evidence of the jewelry box. While he showered, several proposal ideas ran through his head. *I should've proposed on the private jet, that would've been dope. Wait maybe I can do it on a day cruise, or dinner. What if she doesn't like the ring? She'll like it. What if she says not now? She might not say yes, oh God. If she doesn't say yes, I'll kill her.* He laughed as soap suds and water ran down his face. He knew she wanted to marry him, he was just getting nervous. He stepped out of the shower and slipped on an oversized bath robe, rolled his clothes into a tight ball and walked into the room.

Ja'Bria dove into the plush white down comforter and snuggled between the pillows. She had the biggest smile on her face as she dreamed of Omar proposing to her. They were celebrating their anniversary but this time it was different. They were traveling in such a luxurious way that she couldn't imagine anything other than the perfect proposal.

"Get dressed, let's take a walk on the beach and find something good to eat" Omar said as he started unpacking his suitcase. "What should I wear?" she asked as grabbing her luggage and rolling it towards the chase lounge chair. "It doesn't matter, I think Ja'Bari and Tatiana should be here around 10 tonight. We'll do the big dinner then" Omar told her as he laid out a pair of khaki cargo shorts and a navy polo shirt. Ja'Bria pulled out a casual navy blue sundress and a pair of flat Chanel sandals. She was so excited to be in Turks & Caicos for the first time.

While she was in the shower, Omar called the concierge desk and asked for dining recommendations near or at the hotel. "Well Sir, you've contacted the right person. We have 21 restaurants to choose from on the resort's property and we have a dining guide downstairs for other restaurants in the area. What type of cuisine are you interested in for the night?" Omar put the phone on speaker and grabbed his toiletries bag. "It doesn't matter, I guess a steakhouse or a seafood restaurant would be great, we like both" Omar said as he looked in the mirror and brushed the waves in his low-haircut. "Do you have any recommendations?" "Absolutely, our restaurant Eleven has the freshest seafood and steak in town! Our Culinary Experts use a special blend of international flavors, spices and techniques to make top of the line meals. Would you like for me to confirm reservations for you all this evening?" the concierge asked with enthusiasm. "Sure, it's 6 o'clock now, let's confirm two people for 7:45 pm" Omar requested as he kicked his feet up and turned on the television...

Ja'Bria ordered steak and prawns with asparagus and mashed potatoes, Omar ordered steak and a lobster tail with rice and green beans. It was by far one of the most beautiful restaurants they had ever seen. "Everything is bomb so far. The jet, the hotel, the guest services, the food, everything" Ja'Bria said as she leaned towards him for a quick kiss. "Move, I had food in my mouth!" Omar said laughing as he quickly swallowed his food and kissed her back.

"So tell me about the private jet, how did that happen?" Ja'Bria asked. "Oh you know my homeboy that helps with video production?" "Yeah, I think so" Ja'Bria lied so he would continue. "He actually gets 50% off all services with them and they have special rates if you book on certain days. Tuesday is a slow day for them I assume, but the roundtrip price was a little less than six thousand and that's with everything included. Your brother and Tatiana are coming back with us" Omar explained. He was quite proud that he even ran into such a great deal. "Oh that's not bad, it would have been almost that much to fly first class probably" she said as she mentally planned their next vacation.

"What if we had never decided to work for ourselves? We wouldn't be able to do half of the things we can do now" Ja'Bria added as she sipped a glass of aged red wine. "You're right, we have a long way to go but we've come so far" Omar agreed as he raised his glass to suggest a quick toast. "To our past, present and future" he smiled.

"We're here, I'll call y'all when we check in and get settled" Ja'Bari called Ja'Bria. Omar and Ja'Bria finished their meal and headed back to their room. The sun had set and the ocean sparkled like glitter. The stars seemed to shine brighter than normal and the moon was a perfect semicircle. They opened the balcony doors and let the breeze flow through the room. The ocean waves calmly crashed against the shore as they stepped onto the balcony. "This is priceless" Ja'Bria declared as she sat on Omar's lap and kissed him endlessly. "I love you" he whispered as they went back into the room and got into the bed. They continued kissing as they pulled at one another's clothes. Just as Ja'Bria pulled her dress over her head her phone rang. "I've been calling y'all, we've been in the room waiting on y'all. What's the move?" her twin brother asked. "Sleep Bari, sleep!" she said as she ended the call.

Ja'Bari looked at his phone with a screwed face for a few seconds, "They're sleeping or something, are you hungry?" he asked Tatiana as they stretched across the bed. "Sure, let's get something quick" Tatiana suggested as she hopped off the bed. They both took quick showers and headed down to find a bar.

Cliché

"Do you know what today is? It's our anniversary, our anniversary" Tony Toni Tone's song played as Omar wrapped his arms around Ja'Bria from behind and swayed from side to side, kissing her on the neck. She smiled and danced along with him. "I love you" she whispered. "I love you more" he whispered back. Ja'Bari rolled his eyes and shook his head laughing while Tatiana giggled, "aww how sweet".

They were on a luxurious dinner cruise. The staircase was ivory with golden rails and sat in the center of the main lobby of the boat. There were large statues of golden lions at the beginning of the staircase, and the floors were cream colored with golden flakes. The dimly lit chandelier provided the perfect atmosphere and love was in the air.

As the song ended, Omar walked towards the dinner buffet. He discretely pulled the ring out of his pant pocket, glanced at it and quickly shoved the box back into his pocket. Ja'Bria watched him; she was so excited she could hardly wait. She raised the bottom of her long dress, tipped towed towards Omar and asked him what he was doing. He shook his head nervously, "nothing, why?" "Just wondering" she smiled. For some reason he became uncomfortable and walked away. Ja'Bria looked confused and decided to give him his space. *I can't do this, fuck this, what if she's not the one? What if I meet the love of my life 5 months from now? Besides, she irritates me when she gets all mushy, hell nah. I'm not doing it.* Omar thought to himself as he rapidly fixed a second plate of food. Strawberries and cantaloupe fell off his plate as he grabbed a roll of silverware.

"Man I can't do it. I don't know what I was thinking. I'm not ready for this yet" Omar declared as he sat at the table beside Ja'Bari. "Come on man, my sister really loves you. Besides, you're the only dude I will let her date. You gotta do it" Ja'Bari continued, shaking his head. He became a little irritated so he excused himself from the table.

What's wrong baby? You seem uncomfortable about something" Ja'Bria questioned as she sat at the table where her brother had just left. "Nothing man, I'm good. Go have fun with Tatiana or something, I'm just chillin' " he said as he rolled his eyes. Ja'Bria looked confused for a second and decided to play him at his own game. "Okay, well fuck you too Omar" she calmly said, leaving her plate behind. She walked over to the stairwell and sat at the bottom staring off into space. She realized that he was getting 'cold feet' about proposing to her. She wanted to see the ring but she didn't want to push him away even further by being clingy.

"Blackjack!" Ja'Bria yelled as she collected 2,000

points worth of chips. The blackjack table was lit, a beautiful white woman sat beside Ja'Bria and sparked up a long skinny cigarette. As she blew the cigarette smoke away from Ja'Bria with her perfectly tinted red lips, she struck up a conversation. "What do you do for a living?" "I'm in cosmetology school, but I own a clothing store in a contemporary area in Atlanta. I'm a celebrity fashion stylist. What do you do if you don't mind me asking?" Ja'Bria responded. "Well, I'm the Chief Designer at Bebe, our corporate office is in California. We need some fresh new ideas and designs, you seem to have a unique and classy style" the lady smiled. "Blackjack!" The lady yelled as she collected her chips. Ja'Bria looked at the blackjack table for a few moments, it was the perfect time to talk to someone in the fashion industry. "Here take my business card, let's chat whenever you get a chance." The lady handed her a business card and extended her hand. "Lisa", "Ja'Bria", they shook hands and smiled. "Well good luck over here, I'm about to shoot some dice!" "Lisa" walked away. Ja'Bria admired her black silk gown and mink shawl. She wore a beautiful set of pearls with a small diamond in the middle with a pair of earrings to match.

Ja'Bria cashed in her chips and ran towards Tatiana, "girl, the Chief Designer at Bebe just introduced herself to me, gave me her business card and told me to call her! She liked my style." "Girl shut up! That's big, make a note in your cell phone to email her tomorrow and thank her for taking the time out to introduce herself yata, yata, yata" Tatiana suggested as she quickly hugged Ja'Bria. "That's big business, would you take a job if they offered it to you?" "If they let me be an independent contractor and work with them instead of for them, yes" Ja'Bria said firmly. "I know that's right girl, go for it, you don't have anything to lose."

The girls went out on the deck of the boat and ended up with champagne glasses in their hands. "I've never had an evening mimosa, interesting!" Tatiana giggled as she sipped. "I know right?" Ja'Bria agreed as she chugged the last bit of OJ and champagne. "You know my temp job ended last week, but that ended up being perfect because here we are in Turks & Caicos! Your brother is so good to me, I hope we last forever like you and Omar" Tatiana wished, gazing into the ocean. "Here grab a seat." Ja'Bria pulled a lounge chair over for Tatiana. "So spill the beans, this trip is for Omar to propose to me isn't it?" "Well, yeah I think so" Tatiana answered not wanting to give away the surprise. "I knew it!" Ja'Bria said smiling, "have you seen the ring yet?" "Noooo!" Tatiana honestly stated. "Just wait and see" she added. "So when is he doing it?" Ja'Bria asked. "I'm not sure, it seems like he was supposed to do it tonight but don't quote me because Ja'Bari never told me that." "Omar is acting hella weird tonight, I saw him peek at the ring and then he started being distant. I think he's getting scared" Ja'Bria said as she looked down at her new Furla pumps. "Let's go back inside" Tatiana suggested as they grabbed their clutches and sat their empty glasses down.

"The night is far from young, can I have this dance before we port?" Ja'Bari clasped Tatiana's hand. "Of course you can" she smiled leaning forward for a quick kiss. "Omar is trippin'. I should've known he'd back out but oh well, like I said that's on them." He leaned forward and whispered in her ear. "You're next if you act right and I'm a man of my word." Goosebumps covered Tatiana's spine as she leaned back to look at him, "how have I been so far?" *Baby you're my everything, you're all I ever wanted...* Drake's 'Best I ever Had' dropped right on time. "My thoughts are blasting through the speakers right now hahaha." "Ohhh I liked that big bear hug! Give me another one." Tatiana cooed leaning her head on Ja'Bari's chest. "I feel so safe in your arms, baby please don't ever change on me." Swaying from side to side and holding each other tight, they savored the moment.

Honkkkk Honkkkk Honkkk the ships horn sounded off while approaching the shore. "Finally, that was the scariest moment ever man. I almost proposed to my girl and I am not ready." Omar leaned over and started a conversation with a younger man who was there with his family. "I'd wife her up, is that your girl over there looking lonely?" "Yeah that's her, why did you say she looks lonely?" "Look at her man, treat her right or somebody else will. Not sure how her personality is but from the looks of things she's a winner. You won't be the last person to think about marrying her, she'll eventually move on man, go for it." The young man nodded his head out of respect and excused himself from the table.

"Ahh yes, Parrot Cay?" Ja'Bari sat in the passenger seat of an uber SUV and confirmed that it was the right driver while Tatiana, Ja'Bria and Omar sat in the back. "Y'all are too quiet, say something, anything" Tatiana demanded. "I was so sure that this was the night you were going to propose to me, I mean we've talked about marriage and I thought you were just as ready as I am." Ja'Bria sat in the third row of the SUV and curled up in the corner. "I'm not sure I'm ready for all of this Ja'Bria. Can you imagine if we got married and started to hate each other? I mean seriously, all of my friends that are married are miserable and I'd rather keep things the way they are." "Maybe you have the wrong friends, I can't wait to marry Tatiana," Ja'Bari admitted with confidence. "Okay, well do you want to buy this ring? Here it is, I'm not doing it!" Ja'Bari pierced Omar with his eyes while stretching to look towards the back seat. "You are a coward, hell no I don't want to buy the ring that was supposed to be my sister's. It's slick disrespectful so I'll let you blow that steam off by yourself." "How is that disrespectful? I'll sell it to you for cheaper than what I paid for it and besides I haven't seen you make any plans to marry Tatiana." "First of all fuck cheap! Second, I won't punk out when I decide to make that commitment. Third, I'm trying to enjoy my vacation so fuck you and your weak ass feelings for the rest of the trip. Y'all can sort that shit out on your own. Bria call me if you need me." The uber driver arrived at the resort just in time. Ja'Bari paid with his phone, gave the driver five stars and abruptly got out. "Wait Ja'Bari!" Tatiana rushed behind him. "Sorry dude rubbed me the wrong way, I just want my sister to be happy." "I know and she will be." The tension in the air was so thick you could slice it with a knife. Omar stepped onto the elevator without acknowledging Ja'Bria and she stood as far away from him as she could while they rode in complete silence. The lump in her throat somehow blocked the tears from flowing and his nonchalant attitude added pain and regret to her thoughts. *I can't wait to get back home, I'm packing my things and leaving. I'm so glad this happened now instead of later. Ugh, look at him. Cocky ass hole.* Ja'Bria shook her head as she stepped off the elevator. She shoved the hotel room door open and stormed in without holding it for him to follow. He caught the door and mumbled under his breath. "What? What did you just say? Fucking coward." She stood directly in front of him and shoved him. "Say it out loud, don't be scared now, you've done the worst thing you could do. You humiliated me and you made me feel like the scum of the earth. Words won't hurt a bit so say it again." "You'd better keep your fucking hands to yourself or else. I didn't hit you so don't hit me." He firmly said swelling up as if he was going to react. "Or else what!?" She shoved him again as he grabbed her wrists and squeezed them until she became too weak to continue. "Calm down, I still love you. I'm just not ready and you can't force me to be. We've come too far for you to act like this man just please chill out." He leaned forward to kiss her. "Get the fuck away from me! I don't even know who you are anymore and I don't really want to know." She snatched away from him and collapsed in the chair by the window. No longer holding back her tears, she let out the most pain filled sigh Omar had ever heard. "Ohh no don't do this baby. Just because I didn't propose tonight doesn't mean I won't propose at all. Let's enjoy our vacation and see what happens." "You said it yourself, you're not ready. Just leave me alone, I want to be by myself" she calmly cried. "Alright I'll leave you alone for now but just know I love you. Tell me you love me too" he said softly kneeling in front of her. "You tried to sell my ring to my brother. Just leave Omar please, just leave." She turned away from him and stared out of the window. She grabbed her kindle and the half full bottle of red wine from the night stand, poured herself a glass and buried herself in the covers. She opened "Sleeping in Sin" by Cornelia Smith and sipped her wine. *What in the world! Oh this is getting good, I can't go to sleep until I find out what happens next.* She chuckled as she poured the last bit of wine in her glass and read until she eventually dozed off.

Love, oh Love

"Dear God, thank you for waking me up to another day" Ja'Bria robotically whispered as she rolled over to see the sunrise. It was beautiful, she was so blessed to even have the lifestyle she once dreamed of, however she couldn't understand why Omar backed out of the proposal. She didn't want to ruin her vacation by worrying about something that she had no control over, but she felt in her heart that he wasn't going to propose anymore.

"Mar, wake up. Look at the sunrise, it's the most beautiful thing I've ever seen. Look baby, look!" She shook him to wake him up. "What? You've seen the sunrise a million times, go back to sleep." He snatched away and rolled over. Tears streamed down Ja'Bria's face as she walked over to the chase lounge chair and snuggled in her fleece robe.

She stared out of the window and reflected on where she once was. She envisioned herself crying as she walked out of one of her call center jobs, and struggled to get another. She thought about how hard it was to keep the amount of food stamps she was approved for, how hard of a fight she had to put up just to get unemployment insurance, then she smiled. *God doesn't make mistakes, he makes upgrades. Thank you Lord!*

With her final thoughts, Ja'Bria jumped off the chair with excitement. She wanted to take a stroll on the beach alone and continue watching the sky change colors. She slipped her sundress on from the day before, brushed her teeth, fingered her hair into a quick bun, slipped on her flat sandals, washed her face and headed downstairs. "Care for a complimentary cup of coffee or breakfast?" one of the resort staff members asked her as she stepped off the elevator. "I'll take a cup of coffee please" she smiled. "Right this way ma'am" the nice lady said as she motioned with her hands into a ball room area. The breakfast buffet was set up so elegantly. They had four types of coffee to choose from along with different creamers, sugar and sugar substitute. "Wow, you all have everything don't you?" Ja'Bria smiled at the hotel staff member. "We have quite a selection, help yourself." After making a cup of coffee and grabbing a banana-nut muffin, Ja'Bria was on her way to the beach.

She stuck her earbuds in and let her Ashanti Pandora station roll out the hits. One of her favorite songs popped up as her feet hit the sand, "I'm so – happy – baby." She sang as she bopped towards the ocean. She felt an extreme sense of appreciation for the white sand and the warm ocean water, things that she only imagined she'd be able to see. The best thing about it, Ja'Bria knew, if by chance Omar didn't want to marry her, someone else more remarkable would. She reminded herself that she was an amazing woman and the world was at her fingertips.

"Where are you?" Omar called and asked her with a slight attitude. "I'm at the beach, they have a crazy buffet downstairs if you're hungry" she said in a chipper tone. "Why are you so damned jolly at 8:30 in the morning?" he asked rolling out of bed. "Because I'm blessed. Why should I be sad and bent out of shape because you backed out on proposing to me?" she asked, catching an attitude back with him. "Man what? You trippin'' he said as he hung up the phone. Her feelings were hurt for a slight second and she reminded herself what Omar won't do, someone else will.

Omar looked out of the window to see if he could spot her on the beach anywhere. He was pissed that she called him out. *Man Ja'Bari talks too much, nah he probably didn't tell her. But how did she know I was going to propose on this trip? We have been together forever. It seems like when people get married they stop having the perfect relationship. That's what all my married homies say...* Omar paced back and forth across the hotel room as he became uncomfortable with the idea that someone else might come along and scoop Ja'Bria off her feet if he didn't step up. *Who's going to take her on a private jet and buy her expensive shit, tell her not to worry about anything, her money is her money? She ain't going nowhere. Besides, she's already put in too much work with me.* Omar knew he wanted to propose but he was too trifling to give up his selfish ways.

"Why didn't you call me back?" He called Ja'Bria again. "You hung up" she giggled as she rinsed her feet at a beach sprinkler. Her jolly mood was annoying the shit out of him because he was battling with his own issues. "Look, I'll be back up there in a little while. Do you want some breakfast or anything while I'm out?" "No, I'm good. I was thinking we should go snorkeling or something today" he said as he relaxed a little. "That's cool, I'm down for whatever. I'll see you when I get back up there." Ja'Bria hung up. She texted Ja'Bari and Tatiana and asked if they were up yet. Tatiana called and told her she was downstairs grabbing breakfast. "I think your brother is still sleep or just waking up. What are you doing?" she asked. "Coming back in from walking the beach, girl I had to get my mind right." Ja'Bria and Tatiana laughed in unison. "I feel you girl. So what are we doing after breakfast?" Tatiana asked as she covered Ja'Bari's plate with napkins and neatly stacked hers on top. "I don't know, Omar wants to go snorkeling or something. Find out what Ja'Bari wants to do and let me know." She shivered from walking back into the cold hotel. "I' m about to check out this gift shop and I'll be back in my room. Hit me up."

Ja'Bria grabbed a journal with a picture of the beach, at the bottom it read *"Footprints from Turks and*

Caicos…" She loved it so she grabbed it along with a matching ink pen. "I think I'll start a journal while I'm here" she smiled at the clerk and handed over her credit card. "Well that's a fine idea" the clerk smiled and handed Ja'Bria her card back. Even though Omar said he wasn't hungry, Ja'Bria figured it wouldn't hurt to grab him a few of his favorite things. She fixed a plate of fruit for them to share and another plate with turkey sausage, eggs and French toast.

"Good morning boo" she called out as she opened the door. Omar threw his phone on the bed as if he were doing something sneaky. Ja'Bria looked at him sideways and raised her eyebrow but she didn't address it. "Good morning. You got up and out early today" he said as he sat all the way up so to eat. "I couldn't sleep so I decided to enjoy the sunrise alone since you didn't want to watch it with me. It's so peaceful out there, it's not like any other beach we've ever been to." She gazed out the window for a split second. "I know, that's why I brought you here." He leaned forward to kiss her. "Ew! Did you brush your teeth?" she asked him, playfully mushing his face away. "Did you wash your ass?" he laughed as he playfully kissed her on her cheek and neck tickling her. "Stop, okay, okay" she giggled as she climbed on the other side of the bed. She picked up his phone to see if he would get worked up. He looked at her the whole time but didn't say anything.

She just placed the phone on the nightstand beside her. "Why would you put it right there?" He asked as he laid a towel on the bed so they could eat breakfast. "It was in the way, you want it?" she asked with an attitude. "I'm good, you are crazy as hell, you know that right?" he began eating his food. "You're crazier for not proposing to me" she said. She was ready to press the issue one last time before letting it go. "Man look, I have so many friends who are married and miserable. They all say that once you get married everything changes" Omar looked her in the eyes. "Some people never get married and they live happily ever after. I don't know what the big deal is anyway." He shook his head. "Besides, how did you know I was thinking about proposing? I mean how do you know I even want to get married?" "Are you serious? We've talked about this a million times or more. Look, if you don't want to get married, let me know because I do and I can move the hell on." Ja'Bria slid the plate of fruit towards him. She opened her suitcase and searched for something to wear for the day. "No baby, it's not even that. I just don't want to mess up something so perfect." "How can that mess it up? Marriage will only get us prepared for children and I'm not getting any younger." She snatched her flat iron out of her suitcase. "Woah, calm down girl. I know that but I have kids already and besides you don't know how hard it is to even go through marriage. The whole thing gets so annoying that it turns you off." "Okay Omar, then why in the hell did you buy a ring!? Huh? What the fuck was that for?" she asked as she snatched his pants off the closet door from the night before. She looked through both pants pockets but when she didn't find it, she felt sort of embarrassed so she asked him where the ring was. "First of all, how do you know that I even bought a ring?" "Omar I saw you take it out of your pants and look at it! Do you know how fucking sad I was when I realized that you weren't going to ask me?" Tears streamed down her face as she heavily walked into the bathroom. Once the water got steamy, she stepped in and let it hit her hot puffy face. She cried for a few moments longer before she washed her tears away and continued bathing. Omar just sat there; he sort of felt bad and he sort of felt non-apologetic. The last thing he wanted to do is feel pressured into doing something he wasn't sure he wanted to do.

Under the Sea

Ja'Bria grabbed Omar's hand as she swam towards a chest, it looked just like they do on movies. She pointed and muffled "look! Let's see if there's some gold or jewels!" She laughed as she played in the treasure chest. She pulled out a pearl necklace and moved a large rock from the middle. "Girl leave that alone!" Omar said laughing as he grabbed her hand and swam away from the box. They saw a school of beautifully colored fish, a few starfish, jellyfish and more interesting sea creatures before going back to shore.

"How was scuba diving?" Tatiana asked as she plopped down on her bed. The guys were out having beers and the girls were having girl talk in the hotel room. "It was fun, we saw a lot of things that you hear about and see on TV" Ja'Bria laughed. "Oh that's pretty cool. We went to a mall about 5 miles from the hotel. Girl they had a few nice stores but it's pretty expensive so we didn't get much. I got this cute dress and these sunglasses, that's it." Tatiana showed Ja'Bria. "Oooh that's real cute!" Ja'Bria grabbed the dress and held it up to herself. "Thanks girl, so what do you think about Omar backing out on the proposal?" Tatiana asked. "I'm cool with it, I know that if he never does, somebody will. Who would let all of this go over an ego?" She profiled her curves in the mirror. The girls laughed and Ja'Bria joined Tatiana, stretching across the bed. They surfed channels for a few minutes and decided to order room service.

***

"I didn't expect to stay out this long. Man, she is mad fly" Ja'Bari said as he checked out a beautiful caramel chick whose hair was layered with big curls and burgundy highlights. Her red dress looked as if it were painted on and her curves were perfect. "Man, that ain't fair. You can check out girls everywhere we go, but I can't, cause I go with your sister. Not a good look" Omar joked as he slightly shoved Ja'Bari. "Do your play boy, but hurt my sister and that's your life" Ja'Bari joked back. "Let's head back to the room. Do you think the girls want to go out tonight?" "I know Tatiana probably doesn't, Ja'Bria probably doesn't either but we can ask."

"Wake y'all asses up!" Ja'Bari shouted walking into his hotel room. The girls were laid out across the bed with trays of food at the foot of the bed. "It's our last night, we need to turn up!" Omar added slapping Ja'Bria with a down pillow. She looked frazzled for a moment and jumped up and grabbed a pillow and hit him back. Ja'Bari grabbed a pillow and hit Ja'Bria defending Omar and Tatiana grabbed a pillow and hit Ja'Bari defending Ja'Bria. They were all striking each other with pillows after a while and before they knew it, feathers were flying and they were laughing like children.

Hip-hop nightlife, delicious tapas, VIP sections and drink specials – this is a night club you don't want to miss! Tatiana read on a travel blog. Since she and Ja'Bria had agreed to go clubbing they tried to find the best club on the island. "Look at this one, it's like three miles from here, the pictures look nice." "Cute, what other clubs are listed?" "You don't sound too hyped about this, let me see…" Ja'Bria scrolled down the page. "This isn't a club, they say it looks more like a lounge but it's cute! They still have VIP sections and bottles. They also have a night menu oooh with lamb chops, lobster tails, spinach and artichoke dip and so on." She scanned through the pictures. "Oooh, now that's my speed." Tatiana grabbed the laptop and read the reviews. "Well I wasn't really looking for something that we would like, the boys want to go out not us." She stiffly rolled her eyes. "Why you rolling your damned eyes? It is not that serious, here take your lil' laptop before I get an attitude." Tatiana turned the television on and proceeded to ignore Ja'Bria. "Well whatever bitch you'll get over yourself in a minute." Tatiana didn't respond she just flipped through the channels pretending to care what they watched. "Oh this is nice! They have a patio that opens up to the beach with an outside bar, they have a club indoors!"

Ja'Bria said after a long commercial break of silence. "Let me see." Tatiana slid the computer towards herself. "It is nice! Look at the fire pit by the beach." Her eyes lit up. "Cool, we'll go here!" Ja'Bria was happy they came to a mutual agreement. Meanwhile, the fellas were on the balcony drinking local beer and playing cards.

"What time are we leaving? It's already seven o'clock" Tatiana leaned out to ask Ja'Bari. "I guess we can get there around eleven. Tell Bria to start getting dressed now!" he chuckled. "Yeah man she does take forever to get ready, just to look like she always does" Omar tried it. "Watch your mouth little dude, watch your mouth." Ja'Bari warned as he threw the cards on the table, "tunk". He left Omar to join his sister and girlfriend. "I'll start getting ready in about an hour with your smartass mouth." Ja'Bria playfully gave Ja'Bari an old school blooper. "Oooh you got me, go ahead now hahaha." "Okay I'm going back up to our room to chill for a minute and start getting ready." "I'm coming too." Omar walked in from the balcony. "The flights are five seventy-nine on the way back." Omar nudged Ja'Bria. "Okay, why are you telling me?" she asked as she sucked her teeth and crawled out of bed. I can't believe he's acting like everything is normal. He didn't even bother to say we're not going back on a private jet or anything. Guess I'm just not worth it.... Ja'Bria tried to make sense of what all seemed so perfect less than a week prior to her current situation. She reminisced about a book she read in school, "Things Fall Apart" when her thoughts were interrupted by Omar. "Pack your stuff man, I think we'll leave around 8 o'clock tonight. You got your card so I can book your flight?" Ja'Bria snapped at him, "You brought me here, you buy my ticket back, what the fuck do you think this is!?" "Woah pit-bull slow down, I was just asking." He responded as he back into the room and decided not to take the conversation any further.

Ja'Bria took a shower and got dressed to walk the beach one last time. *"They talkin' real loud, but we mute that, and I'm killin' all these hoes where the news at?"* She bopped her head to Bambi's mixtape as she walked towards the boardwalk and the more crowded area of the beach. "One pina colada in a big coconut please." "Here you go, first one's on the house," the man serving fresh drinks offered. "Thanks!" She decided to post up at an umbrella nearby as she watched the ocean waves crash and smelled the fresh breeze of the beach while she listened to her favorite jams. *Your flight is booked, we are leaving the hotel around 7:30 just FYI.* Omar texted Ja'Bria. She didn't respond, it was 12 o'clock noon and her suitcase was packed minus the dress she was wearing and the one she had laid across the sofa to wear home.

"Hey girl! I thought I'd find you down here." Tatiana skipped towards Ja'Bria. Although she didn't want to be bothered, she took her headphones out and smiled as they talked about their vacation and plans once they got home.

#WORK

"You know I got you boss, give me a breakdown of all of the overhead costs and we'll go from there." Rapper Young Boss said to Omar as they reviewed the paperwork for the video shoot. "It's only $12,500 for everything. You know nobody else can get all of this for the low like that" Omar told the young rapper. Omar was a high profile videographer and editor for music videos and special occasions. He was plugged in with some major social media sensations so they always reposted his pictures and music from his clients which provided extra exposure. Ja'Bari is a part-time realtor and he owned an exotic car dealership. Omar was able to shoot incredible videos with the resources at hand. He usually split everything with Ja'Bari when they were using his homes and cars. The business could be annoying at times because middle men and third parties could become sticky, but there's nothing too hard for a boss to handle, right? "Look man, we can only shoot the video for 4 hours. Nobody is spending all day and they can't come up with all of the money. We need one hitter quitters today, that's it" Ja'Bari told Omar. "I know, I got you. They're shooting at the park too, but I'll make sure you get your car back on a full tank and I'll get it detailed too" Omar promised as he stapled a few papers together and placed them into a manila folder. Ja'Bari rolled his eyes, "Two hours, fuck them young ass boys man." "Three" Omar bargained. "Two hours and forty-five minutes, bring my shit back" Omar laughed. "Alright man, we're on our way to the house now. Get dressed, I'll be there in about thirty minutes to scoop you."

'Ballin' like hoopers on the NBA courts nigga, smoking the best weed with the baddest bitches, pullin' triggas'. Young Boss rapped as the footage was being recorded. They were recording at the swimming pool. There were a few video vixens in swimsuits, Young Boss's entourage and a pit bull standing at the double doors that lead to the house. Ja'Bari laughed and rolled his eyes, "I hate these lil dudes I swear." He went into the house to make sure everything was spotless. They didn't record inside because it was empty so they made good use of the exterior. They went to the front and recorded Young Boss hopping in a lime green Lamborghini and pulling out of the driveway. "He wants to be Jeezy so bad, get him out of here. Bring the Lambo back in better condition than it's in right now" Ja'Bari said laughing. "Bet, I'll holla at you in a few" Omar called out as they cut the scene.

Omar and the rest of his filming crew packed their equipment and headed to the next location. *#SWYD and come show love at my video shoot! #Models #G's #LezzGetIt.* Young Boss posted a picture of himself leaning against the Lambo beside the Grant

Park sign on Instagram. Within 30 minutes the park was at least 300 people deep. Weed smoke filled the air, Hennessey bottles were continuously being popped and Young Boss rapped about how "real" he is...

About an hour later, blue and red lights flew around the corner. "Alright wrap it up!" one of the police officers demanded over an intercom. Some people scattered, some finished their blunts and drinks rapidly and some stood there defiantly, Young Boss and his entourage. "Can't you see I'm having a video shoot over here?" Young Boss walked over to the cop smelling like a pound of weed. "Sir, there were no reservations to rent out this park and illegal activity is being conducted. Atlanta Police Department is lenient with a lot of things but if you all don't leave the premises, we will take action. Try us." The officer threatened as he shifted his weight to one leg and tapped his handcuffs. Young Boss walked away and yelled "Fuck twelve!" Another police officer jumped out of his police car and followed him. "Excuse me sir?" Young Boss unlocked the door to the Lamborghini and sat in the driver seat, "What man, I'm just trying to shoot my video. Y'all always fucking with somebody." He lit a clove and blew smoke in the officer's face. "Okay, that's it, step out of the car with your hands behind your head" the officer said as he snatched the handcuffs off his belt. "You little disrespectful fucker. You got people smoking pot, drinking in a public park, popping God knows what kind of pills and you want to say fuck us? No, fuck you, fucking bastard." The officer spoke while he was cuffing the young man. "Are you going to read me my Miranda rights or nah, punk ass police?" Young Boss asked as he looked over his shoulder. "Mar, y'all get this on camera!" he yelled to Omar. Omar zoomed in and out of the scene for a few shots of Young Boss getting handcuffed before his camera battery started going dead. "Alright, I got it my battery is going dead now" Omar told him. As his heart started racing, Omar pulled out the paperwork that he and the rappers signed earlier. "Print the warrant, he's a smart ass" the cop said over a walkie-talkie. "Warrant for what!?" Young Boss asked nervously. I don't have any warrants and my record is clean man don't fuck with me like that." His eyes teared up. "This is fucked up on so many levels." He started getting nervous. "It's a warrant to search the vehicle, chill out." The officer shoved Young Boss towards the hood of the car. "Stay right there for a minute while we search this car." They snatched the glove compartments opened, the console, looked under the mats, and got a police dog to go behind them. The dog went to the trunk and started barking. Young Boss didn't have a care in the world, he knew the car was clean and so was he. All they could possibly pin on him was less than a half of an ounce of marijuana.

"Look what the fuck we have here. A kilo of cocaine, eight pounds of weed, and a half kilo of heroine. Is that how you're paying for this hot ride Mr. Johnson?" The cop said as he looked over Young Boss's Driver's License. "Man that's not mine! Y'all planted that on me man hell nah!" Young Boss pleaded, "This can't be real man hell nah, I know, I'm being punked?" "Lock him up, pull the dealerships info and his entire record." The officer then pushed Young Boss into police the car.

Young Boss felt like everyone had left. In reality, everyone was still at the park but he didn't see them in his peripheral so he felt as if it were him vs. the cops. "Where is everybody at man?" Young Boss asked as he leaned over and looked out of the window. He saw Omar standing far off to the side on the telephone. The cameras were still rolling, he started thinking that it would be good publicity although the drugs weren't his. He smiled and realized that he was going to use this to his advantage, maybe even gain a bit of street credit if possible. After the Police Officer spoke to Omar for a few moments, they drove Young Boss to the county jail and set his bond at three hundred thousand dollars.

"He can pay his bond or sit in there, it's only three thousand dollars. I can refer him to a bails bondsman. I'm not his manager, dad or baby sitter" Omar said, speaking to Young Bosses friend on the phone. "I feel you but he feels like this is your fault, like somehow maybe you or your people had something to do with the shit in the car." "Was it us or was it the cops? He has to stick to what he thinks or nobody is going to believe him, at least not me." Omar said in defense. "Alright man, just let me know if anything changes. He doesn't have three hundred thousand dollars for no damn bond either, you know that." Young Bosses friend said in mere disappointment. "He'll pay three thousand with the bail bondsman, they only need ten percent." Omar informed the young boy before they ended the conversation.

Irresponsible

"Where is the car Omar?" Ja'Bari asked as it had been over four hours since he had seen the car or heard anything. "Man you won't believe what this lil idiot did." Ja'Bari raised his eyebrow and began to pour himself a small shot of Cognac to keep calm. "What Omar?" "They were smoking during the video shoot, they invited all these people, they were drinking and everything; it was lit out there…" Omar started. "Where the fuck is the car Omar, I don't care about any of that other shit." Ja'Bari got extremely irritated. "The cops seized it because there were drugs in the trunk." Omar cut to the chase. "Drugs? Drugs! What the fuck were they doing with drugs Omar!?" Ja'Bari paced back and forth between the kitchen and the back patio. "The kids think it was your shit, they swear they didn't have anything to do with the drugs Bari." "Oh wow, so somehow I have something to do with this bullshit!? This is the last time I do business with you and these little idiots. The cops better not call me, pop up at my shit or chop my got damned car, if they do that's your ass! I want my car back by 7 AM tomorrow, I don't give a fuck what you gotta do." Ja'Bari was irate, he hung up the phone and turned it off.

"Baby, sit down. What's wrong, talk to me."

Tatiana said as she rubbed his head and sat on his lap. "Move bae, not right now." He said as he slid her off of his lap. She looked confused for a second. "What did Omar do now?" She asked. "This lil dude." Ja'Bari shook his head and palmed his face. "He got a three hundred thousand dollar car tied up in some bullshit with the cops. Some rappers rented the shit but I'm holding him fully responsible, those are his flugazy ass clients." Tatiana shook her head and started taking food out of the refrigerator to cook. He lit a cigar and puffed it while he stared at the ceiling. "My sister needs to get rid of his sloppy ass, I swear, I can't take it anymore. I'm actually glad his punk ass got too scared to ask her to marry him. I definitely won't approve of it, and since our dad passed away, she wouldn't have anyone to walk her down the aisle." Ja'Bari put the cigar in the ashtray and walked over to the couch. "You don't mean that baby, calm down, you're upset." Tatiana chopped a few peppers and onions. "Shit, I'm two seconds from pistol whipping his punk ass." Ja'Bari stretched his legs out. Tatiana pulled out a bowl of marinated beef tips and brushed a few of the finely chopped onions into the warmed olive oil. Once the onions were caramelized, she dumped the beef tips into the pan and began cooking them. "Just chill out, you know what you gotta do. He's stunting your growth and we can't have that around here." Tatiana washed her hands and walked over to comfort her man.

Ding-Dong… Tatiana looked over at Ja'Bari, who had fallen asleep. She checked on the cornbread and walked down the hallway and into the foyer of their home. "Who is it?" she asked as she tried to look through the stained window on the door. "Bria". Tatiana opened the door. "Hey girl come in". They gave each other a hug and walked back into the kitchen. Ja'Bria sat on the stool on the other side of the sink. "You got it smelling good in here girl, what are you cooking?" "Beef tips, rice, cabbage and cornbread. Come help me with the cabbage." Tatiana pulled out a chopping board. Ja'Bria walked into the kitchen and washed her hands. "Okay, so give me the tea bitch because your brother is livid." "Pour some wine girl, this is too damn much." Ja'Bria talked as she cut the cabbage in half. "Here's some merlot, cheers. Proceed now I'm anxious." Tatiana began cooking the rice. The beef tips were simmering on low heat and the dinner was almost done.

"So girl! Omar comes in the house, slings some duffle bag full of equipment onto the couch and tells me that my brother set him up. There were drugs in the trunk of the car he rented for his clients' video shoot" Ja'Bria starts. "First of all, we both know that your brother is smarter than that and as far as I know, he doesn't deal with drugs or anything else illegal. Omar is up to some shit, I can feel it in my bones girl. Leave his ass alone!" Tatiana interrupted.

"Girl, I don't know where the drugs came from but he is all mad at me and he's literally acting like I am supposed to take his side and beef with my twin brother. I think fucking not." Ja'Bria pulled the cornbread out of the oven. Tatiana took a long and hard sip of her wine. "Girl what is his malfunction?" She took the top off the rice. Ja'Bria looked at the cabbage and stirred it around. "Girl, I had to leave the house. I'll go grab a few things to throw on tomorrow but I'm staying over tonight." She slipped her shoes off and sat them by the front door. "Girl you have clean underclothes, tights, tees, jeans, everything in that top drawer in the guest bedroom." Tatiana told her. "I figured I had some things here, good!" Ja'Bria sprinkled a little sugar, red crushed pepper flakes and salt onto the cabbage. She stirred it one last time and turned the eye off. "I think that's everything, the cornbread is cool enough to cut now. The girls were ready to eat and gossip. "Tell me anything you want to say before I wake your brother up." Tatiana urged as she took the lemonade out of the refrigerator. "That was it, everything else can be said in front of Bari. You know I love Omar but at this point I just don't know how to feel. I'm pissed, I know that much." They began setting the table for dinner. "Baby wake up, dinner is ready." Tatiana kissed Ja'Bari on his cheek. "Mmm, okay." He looked up at Tatiana's beautiful brown face and just smiled. He had a beautiful woman who was smart, witty, could cook and always had his back no matter what. He sat up and smiled again. "When did you get here?" He asked his sister as he walked over to the dining table. "Oh, y'all set the table and everything? Shit is about to get real. I hope you left that fuck boy at home." He raised his eyebrow looking at his sister. She got up to fix her plate. "I got here about two hours ago. I can't figure out exactly what happened with the rental car but I want it to be over." Ja'Bria poured gravy from the beef tips onto her rice. "Oh it is going to be over at 7:00 AM tomorrow. Either he brings me back my car unharmed, unmarked and unassociated with anything crazy or he's dead. The choice is his." Ja'Bari poured himself a glass of lemonade. "Ahhhh, this is good baby. You used just the right amount of lemons and sugar" he announced dramatically. As Ja'Bria sat down she said "you're not going to kill him." "He is becoming an expensive bill. You know I hate being hot, front street is not where I bang." Ja'Bari blabbed as Ja'Bria started off into space. "Sis, you hear me talking to you?" "I hear you." She didn't know what to think or how to feel anymore. "Can I get a shot of that?" Ja'Bria asked her twin brother, she just wanted to feel numb. "Baby get her a glass please." Tatiana fixed her boyfriend's twin sister a strong shot while she soaked it all in. "Ja'Bari, be honest with me, did you accidently leave that stuff in the trunk?" Ja'Bria asked out of curiosity. "Man hell no! I don't even know where to get all that crazy shit. Whoever the hell it belongs to is wild! I don't want no parts of it. NONE." Ja'Bari was furious that his sister accused him of being a backsliding criminal. She looked at her phone hoping to see a call or text from Omar but there was nothing. One of her friends texted her, *"girl what happened to your brother and O?"* She just turned her cell phone off. She figured if Omar didn't want to talk to her after hours had passed, he didn't want to talk at all. She was nearly fed up with him. He still hadn't told her why he backed out of proposing after he had the ring in his pocket at dinner when they were on vacation. She became dizzy and anxious, "One more shot, I don't mean to drink it all but damn, my nerves..." She stood up and took a long stretch. "It's all good, I'll go get some more if you want. You and your brother are stressed out." Tatiana wiped the kitchen table and swept the floor. "You can help me with these dishes though sister-in-law." Tatiana giggled and hip bumped Ja'Bria. "I guess." She laughed, she wanted the mood to be a little lighter. Dishes and girl talk sounded like a good idea.

Honor

Ding-Dong... The doorbell rang at 6:48 AM. Nobody budged on the first ring. *Ding-Dong, Ding-Dong, Ding-Dong.* The doorbell rang three more times back to back. Tatiana rolled over, "baby, who is at the door so early in the morning?" She slid her house shoes and silk robe on. "It better be my damn car, I really wish they would have taken it to the car lot but whatever." Ja'Bari sat up and stared at the thick wooden bed post at the foot of the bed. "Yeah, go get the door for me." He slipped his basketball shorts and Nike flip-flops.

"Ja'Bari Wilson please." A man said once Tatiana opened the door. "Oh, I'm his fiancé, I can sign for him. What is it?" She saw someone pulling into the driveway with the lime green sports car. "We're here to drop off this vehicle, does it belong to him?" "It's property of the car dealership, yes." Tatiana signed the digital machine. "Thank you, we'll take it to the dealership. Is everything clear?

Everything is okay, right?" She asked without saying too much. "Yes, everything is taken care of. You're good to go." The car delivery guy tilted his hat, smiled and walked away. "Whew, that was easy," Tatiana said as she walked back upstairs. "He had my shit here by 7 AM, I'm surprised but I'm glad. I hope they don't come to my place of business with the questioning bullshit, if they do, that's his ass all over again. I'm still disgusted by that lil dude, ugh."

Ja'Bari walked out of the bedroom. Tatiana brushed her teeth and joined him downstairs as he cooked breakfast. "Go wake up Bria, she needs to be down here with us." Ja'Bari slid the buttered toast in the oven. "Good morning ugly face." Ja'Bria slowly walked down the steps. "You got the same face as me." Her brother joked. "Mimosas?" Tatiana suggested. "Sure, I'll have one. Thanks girl, you have really been making me feel at home since I stepped foot in here yesterday." "Oh girl, stay as long as you want." Tatiana smiled and poured the glasses to the rim. "I don't know when I'm going back home. I don't want to be around him right now." Ja'Bria threw her hair in a bun. "I have to go to cosmetology class today, I almost forgot." She jumped up from the kitchen stool. After getting dressed, she made a quick turkey bacon, scrambled egg and cheese sandwich from the breakfast food. "Alright, be good. Try to stay away from fuck boys for the rest of the week." Her brother joked with her as she laughed and left. Just to ensure she had a good day, she put in an old CD and played Happy Face by Destiny's Child. She sang and bopped her head on her way to school. *Why haven't you been answering the phone? Did your brother get his car this morning? Where did you sleep at last night?* She got text message after text message from Omar. *I didn't feel like talking to you. What do you think? Where do you think I slept???* She was so irritated by everything he had going on with his videography business, after seeing him in a different light, she could feel her feelings slowly drifting. She thought about him not proposing to her again, that was really a big bother to her, she thought about it all of the time. He texted her back, *oh so now you want to be sarcastic, you better be at home this evening when I get there. What are we eating for dinner so I can be ready?* She rolled her eyes and sucked her teeth, she decided that didn't deserve a response.

"What's up man, Ja'Bari, I'm really sorry all of that stuff went down but you don't have to worry about being a part of it. I think the investigation is pending on Young Boss and his crew." Omar was nervous when Ja'Bari answered the phone. Ja'Bari hardly responded, "Alright" he said and hung up the phone. He just shook his head for a few seconds and walked into the bathroom to run the shower. "What all do you have to do today?" Ja'Bari asked Tatiana. "I think I'm going to this little temp gig for a little while, that's it. What about you?" She asked. "Going to this car lot right now, I'll let you know how everything goes." He stepped into the shower while she brushed her teeth. "Oh, I need you to come get me from the dealership this evening, I have to take that car up there so that's what I'm driving today."

He yelled over the shower. "Okay baby, just let me know. I'm working from 11 to 7 I think." "I need you before 7:30." He replied, he didn't want to be at the dealership all day but he had to make sure it wasn't hot up there. Every time he thought about Omar he became disgusted all over again. "Okay, I'll leave at 6." She rinsed her face off and continued getting ready.

Ohhh, here we go. What the fuck is all of this shit? Ja'Bari thought as he pulled up at the dealership. "What's going on?" he asked as he walked into the dealership. Detectives were questioning random employees, the receptionist, a car salesman and one of the car washers. "There he is, like I said, you need to ask him all of that, I just work here." Ja'Bari's attitude went from zero to one-hundred. "Ask me what man? Fuck all of this extra shit, we weren't affiliated with the illegal portion of yesterday's incidents in any way, shape, form or fashion." He walked into his office and slammed the door. One of the detectives followed him. "Sir, do you know where the drugs came from or who is responsible placing them in the vehicle that belongs to this car dealership?" "Man check the fingerprints, I don't know what else to tell you." Ja'Bari nonchalantly shrugged his shoulders and logged onto his computer. The detective stood in the doorway. Ja'Bari stood up and opened the door as wide as he could and motioned for the detective to excuse himself. He calmly shut the door and sighed, *I should really murder this idiot for making my car lot hot.* He had to figure out a way to keep Omar as far from him as possible forever. He had foolishly crossed him for the last time so he had to cut him off before it was too late if it wasn't already...

He walked back to his desk, sat in the oversized black office chair, swiveled towards the window and kicked his feet up. There was nothing like staring into the crisp blue sky when he couldn't deal with pressure. "Aye, will you please bring me a hot cup of coffee with a few sugar and creams?" He buzzed the front desk. "Here I come, anything else?" The receptionist asked as she stood up and adjusted her pencil skirt. "Yeah man, check the display floor and tell me which two cars are in there. I can't remember shit today. My mind is in a million places." "I bet, I'll be in there in a few. You want your cream and sugar on the side?" "Yeah, thanks Karla." She smiled and nodded as if he could see her. She grabbed a small clipboard with paper and a pen out of an old coffee mug that sat on her desk. She scribbled Red Porsche and walked towards the windshield to see if the VIN number was in the corner. "Good morning, is Ja'Bari available?" A deep voice came out of nowhere, she nearly jumped out of her pumps the man was so close to her. She stepped forward and turned to the side, "He is not available, may I help you?" She answered with a slight attitude. "I asked if he was here." "No, you asked if he was available. May I help you?" She repeated herself this time with a definite attitude. "No, you can't help me with shit. Tell him I'll be back." Omar snapped back as he strolled towards the back of the dealership. "Excuse me sir, where are you going?" She rushed behind him. "To see if I can help myself since you're no good around here." He walked at a faster pace towards Omar's office. She rolled her eyes and rushed over to her desk to page Ja'Bari. "Hey some weird dude is walking towards your office, I told him you weren't available but he walked back there anyway. He's rude!" Karla grabbed her cell phone and slipped it between her boobs in her shirt. "Man, alright." Ja'Bari swiftly walked towards his door and locked it. He sat back down in the same position and stuck his headphones in his ears, he turned to the music shuffler on his phone. *"Young nigga I do my own thing, so let me do it. If you wanna know one thing bout me, I'm bout my paper…"* He rapped along with Wiz Khalifa as he bobbed his head. "Bari let me in man damn, I told you I was gon' handle everything." Karla peeped around the corner and giggled as she walked around the office as if she were just checking on everything. Omar looked through the glass wall and saw Ja'Bari leaned back with smoke blowing in the air. Once he realized Ja'Bari wasn't going to acknowledge him whether he heard him or not, Omar walked away. "What the fuck you looking at?"

He screamed at Karla. "Don't get mad at me, I told you he wasn't available." *"Idiot"* Karla mumbled as she watched him storm through the parking lot and speed off in a black F-150. "Who the fuck was that!?" Karla unlocked Ja'Bari's office and slung it opened. "If you gon have all this shady shit going on, I can leave. I'm trying to stay away from all of that illegal stuff." She shifted her head from side to side while she cursed Ja'Bari out. "Who are you talking to like that?"

He slowly said as he turned to her. She definitely had the looks to keep customers intrigued until they finalized their purchases. She was 22 years old, she stood about 5'4" with a nice figure. She flipped her hair over her shoulder and placed her hand on her hip. "Ja'Bari" she cocked her head to the side waiting for an explanation. "I'm scared to come to work, I'm taking the rest of the month off." She strutted back across the showroom floor as she shoved the clipboard into the desk drawer. "Man chill out, that was my sister's dumb ass ex-boyfriend. Come here." He laughed as he paged her on the office phone. Karla was cute but he already had a girl. There was nothing wrong with having someone who reminded him of his girlfriend and his sister hanging around the office. She was pretty, professional and she had a lot of street smarts. "If you stop chasing those whack ass fake rappers around, maybe you can figure things out. Yo lil crazy ass. Sit down." He said as he finally opened his programs on his computer. She flopped down in the chair across from Ja'Bari. "Nah for real, what was his deal and why was he in here?" She wanted to know as she pulled her cell phone out of her shirt and flip through Instagram. "That's the dumb ass camera dude." Ja'Bari filtered through his unimportant emails. "Oooh. She said as if a light bulb went off in her head." "Yeah oh, I really need one of your lil fly ass homegirls to make friends with his dumb ass and get the scoop on him. I want to know which one of those lil bastards was retarded enough to put drugs in the truck of a quarter million dollar car." Karla's eyes wondered as she thought, "I can link back up with Young Boss, you know I used to talk to him about a year ago. Make him miss me or tell him I miss him, whatever comes first" she smirked. "Alright man, ugh." He laughed. "Shut up! You want me to help you, right?" She questioned with a silly attitude. She liked Ja'Bari as a boss, he was smart and his past was admirable. To see someone who was still somewhat young come from nothing and make something of himself let her know she could do it too, or at least her significant other could once she found one. "Just hang around, try to listen at first and once you're around for a few days, start asking questions if you can fit them into his context. You know what I mean?" He wanted to make sure she understood her role. "Yeah, like I won't be too pushy but at the same time I need to know what the hell is going on. I like my job. I want to keep meeting these rich ass men and prance around the office with nothing much to do." He shook his head, "I'll find something for you to do, stop riding my damn clock. Get out of here." Karla paused. "Look at this post Bari." She handed her phone to him and showed him a post on Instagram. *It's some real snake shit going on but it's all good. We got bail money bitches. #StillBlessed #BossShitOnly #YaDigg*, the caption read. It was a picture of Young Boss standing in front of the mansion that Ja'Bari had on the market and leaning against the lime green Lamborghini while he blew weed smoke in the air. Ja'Bari screenshot the picture and caption and sent it to his phone with no hesitation. He gritted his teeth and breathed heavily. "Why is he posting pictures of my shit all over the internet? I'm never working with set directors again unless they're bringing at least 5 figures to the table." He ranted. Karla looked confused. "Like they didn't even pay a couple of racks to shoot the videos with all of the props?" She turned up her nose, that didn't sound like the Young Boss she knew. He would take her on lavish dates, buy her nice gifts, and always, always look out for his partners. "Why you looking like that?" Ja'Bari asked as he minimized his emails and opened his spreadsheet. "Nothing, he's just not cheap from what I remember." She knew something wasn't adding up but she didn't want to go based on his past. Maybe since he'd tasted a little bit of fame he had changed. She was going to get to the bottom of it because she still had a thing for Young Boss and she was loyal to Ja'Bari.

Rekindle & Swindle

Karla waited a few days until things were a little less intense before she made her initial reconnection. She looked through nearly all of his social media posts and he seemed to be what she was used to. About three days after he posted the shady Instagram message, she went to his page and put a heart eyes emoji under an old selfie he had taken and liked about 40 pictures since he hadn't posted anything all day and surprisingly it worked. He sent her a DM. She smirked, let's see what he got going on. *'Hey stranger what's been going on with you?'* he asked after scrolling through her pictures. *'Good. Kinda miss you.'* She added a winking emoji. *'Word? So you wanna see me or you just gon keep lying about how much you miss me?'* Their DM's were getting quicker, they might as well have been texting *'What do you wanna do?'* *'We can go grab something to eat or whatever you wanna do really.'* *'Cool, just let me know when you're free. My number is still the same.'* *'Aight.'* They ended their messages both feeling excited about linking up. It had been a few years but they didn't end on bad terms. *Keep it together Karla, stick to the script.* She thought to herself as she scrolled through her timeline for a few moments before going to sleep.

Around 4:30 pm Young Boss texted her,

'Karla?' *He still has my number*, she smiled to herself. She waited for about 20 minutes before responding, she didn't want to look desperate. *'Hey what's up? Who's this?'* she texted back. *'8:30 too late for you to do dinner or ya man got you on lock?'* he texted back as he smirked. *'Oh hey boo, I don't have a man why you got a girl?'* she texted as she flipped through the pages of an Elle magazine. *'Nah I'm tryna see what's up with you, I'm single as a dollar bill'* he responded. Work was slow so she was sure she could leave early if she texted Ja'Bari. *'Hey I'm going to dinner so I'm leaving in a few if that's alright with you.'* *'That's cool, try to get the spreadsheets done by 5 on Monday. Have a great weekend'.* *'Cool, you too. Thanks!'* She threw her magazine in the desk drawer and rushed to her car as she told the sales associate to keep an eye on the dealership for the rest of the afternoon. She jumped in her 328i and turned to an old school R&B playlists on her phone. "I'm so into youuu. I don't know what I'm gonna do." She sang to the top of her lungs as she smiled while zipping through traffic. She pulled into the garage at her apartment and started planning what she was going to wear.

After kicking her shoes off at the door mat and throwing her keys on the kitchen countertop, Karla dashed into her room, grabbed a black dress, held it up for a few seconds and laid it on the bed. She didn't want to be too dressy so she grabbed a pair of black skin tight pants, a loosely fitted black v-neck tee shirt and a long loose cardigan with pops of colorful designs. Summertime was nearly ending and the nights felt more like autumn weather. Young Boss called and told her he was in the driveway. She slid on her six inch Jessica Simpson sandals and fastened them, topped off her nude lip glass and slung her Chanel clutch that he'd bought her a few years ago onto her shoulder. She pranced down the hallway with a smirk of confidence as she walked into the apartment's garage.

"You look gorgeous as always." He smiled at her as he leaned over and opened the door. "Not too bad amazing." The soft whiff of cologne was nearly tranquilizing as she leaned back in the plush big body benz seats. He just smiled, "whatever, stop trying to pump my head up girl, you smell good as hell too. We make a good combination if you ask me." "Whatever, enough of the small talk, where are you taking me?" She asked as she adjusted the mirror and checked her hair and make-up.

"It's a surprise." He slightly showed his excitement. She smirked and leaned back again. After an hour of riding Karla became slightly nervous knowing that her true intentions were to get info on a drug scandal. "No seriously, where are you taking me?" She asked firmly. "Don't you trust me?" Young Boss asked laughing. "Maybe, give me a hint." She tried to play it off. "I'll give you a hint alright. Here put this black bandanna over your eyes and don't look." He pulled the bandanna from the back seat and tied it around her head while he steered the car with his left knee. She was scared and excited. "Okay okay!" She relaxed a bit and was ready for the excitement. *What if he knows what I'm doing and he's kidnapping me to keep me quiet? Or what if he wants ransom money. Oh my gosh I hope we're not going to some alley out in bubblefuck nowhere.* Her mind started wondering and her nerves got the best of her so she snatched the bandanna off quickly. "Huhh" she sighed in relief. She looked around for a few moments, she saw a mansion on a huge piece of land which was awkward but a little comforting. "Put the bandanna back on, you are cheating and you gotta trust me. That's two strikes in one. Are we starting our relationship over like this?" He asked as he tied the bandanna back around her eyes. She smiled and said okay showing her excitement. A few minutes later he gently rubbed her face and stole a kiss as he removed the bandanna. She opened her eyes and smiled just enough for her teeth to show. Her face lit up as they slowly drove into the gates of chateau Elan.

"Are you surprised?" he asked as the valet driver walked over to open the doors. "Yes!" She exclaimed walking towards the doors of the restaurant. They ordered a bottle of aged wine and two glasses of water to drink. She ordered the surf and turf dinner with a lobster tail and 6 ounce filet mignon medium well and a vegetable medley, he ordered a T-bone steak well done with whipped potatoes and chives. "This is so nice, what made you come here?" as she gazed at his smooth brown face and deep dimples. "To be honest Karla, I've been thinking about you for quite some time. Sometimes I have flashbacks about us, you were so real and rare. You are nothing like the rest of these girls out here so you deserve something a little better than the average. I didn't think I would ever talk to you again, you just disappeared on me but I guess I deserved it after all of the lies and games I played." He looked away for a moment and looked back at her. "Will you give me a second chance?" He asked as he smiled again. She remembered going through his phone and finding all sorts of crazy text messages. She wasn't so sure she could even be dumb enough to take him serious again. Besides, she was reconnecting with him for a specific reason. She was trying to decide whether she should dog him out like he'd done her or consider giving him another shot because he wasn't the grimy man Ja'Bari thought he was. "I'm talking to you." He interrupted her thoughts. "We'll see, you got some shit with you but we'll see." She agreed to think about it. "I used to, I'm 28 years old now baby, I'm ready to settle down, I just haven't found the one. But I think she was here the whole time." He flashed his dimples again. "If you say so." She laughed. They talked for nearly two hours over dinner reminiscing and catching up.

After dinner, they walked into the hotel and went to the reserved Jr. Suite. "Wow Boss, you've outdone yourself. What do you want in return? I hope you know we ain't doing nothing." She said as she comfortably sprawled across the bed. "I respect that, I just want your time Karla, that's all." He turned on the television and crossed his legs at the foot of the bed as he leaned back on the pure white pillows and linen. He glanced over at her, her head was at the end of the bed as she tuned into the news. "Damn man, that's so messed up." She broke the silence. "I know right, kids getting abducted and don't even get a chance to chase their dreams or live their lives." He replied shaking his head. "Speaking of chasing dreams, you're doing pretty good at it! I'm proud of you... I know you probably hear it all of the time but I've seen you at your beginning stages and you've come a long way." She was genuinely happy for him, he worked so hard at his dreams and she had to commend him for that. "Thank you, I try. So you never told me what you're doing now. You told me how your family and friends are doing, but you didn't say how you're doing. What are you up to these days?" He asked. "I'm a receptionist, nothing major. So, tell me about your next video.

I know it's going to be great!" She quickly changed the subject. "Man, I don't know what to say about it honestly. We shot a video for my new single but we can't drop it on the release date." He rolled his eyes. "Why not?" She asked clueless. "I don't know who to trust anymore. Aye don't ever repeat this but someone set me up. Drugs were in the rentals and the police showed up at the park, locked me up and everything. I really don't want to be wrapped up in that shit but I'll handle it." He huffed a mild sigh of relief, he knew that he could vent to Karla and she would never exploit him. She was always loyal like that. "Wait what the fuck!? What kind of drugs and whose were they?" She asked, *this was easier than I thought it would be.* Although she was concerned about the people around him, she wanted to get to the core of his side quick. "Why are you looking like that?" He asked her as he snatched his neck back. "Like what boo? You're paranoid." She giggled. "Like I said, I don't know who I can trust anymore. I don't know who the drugs belonged to but it wasn't me. The last thing I need is some young dudes thinking it's cool to get caught with that kind of stuff. Besides, that can make me lose out on endorsements and all types of shit. I got too much to lose right now and somebody real close to me obviously got it out for me. I sort of came here to get away from all of that... Can we change the subject?" "Of course we can, let's talk about your intentions with me. Why do you think I'm a good person to pursue right now? You got all this stuff going on and let's be real, I hit you up first." He looked up to the left and thought for a second before he responded. "You were there before any of this shit, when I was paying for studio time instead of getting paid for features. The majority of these females just want my money. You've always had your own or was willing to help me get it." She looked confused, he always spoiled her with nice bags and jewelry and she wasn't the only one. She had a flashback of how unimportant she felt when girls would take to social media and brag about the gifts he bought them, how she would receive random private calls from other girls telling her they were fucking him too and she wasn't important. She could think about these problems all night long but instead she just decided to think with her mind, not her heart. "Why did you get so quiet? I'm for real." He said as he wrapped his arm around her waist. "I'm just dozing off a little bit." She replied as she snuggled close to him. The television was turned off and the windows were opened, they drifted off into the breezy fall night without a single thought of sex. *Knock, knock, knock.* Karla jumped as she looked around confused about where she was. She glanced at the television and remembered watching the news with Young Boss. She slowly rolled out of bed and looked at him as he opened the door, he had ordered room service for breakfast. The crisp and juicy cantaloupe, honey dew melon and grapes garnished the oversized plate, strawberries and pineapples were stacked in the center. They had turkey sausage links, boiled eggs and signature French toast. "Would you like complimentary mimosas?"

The young lady offered as she rolled the cart into the room. "Yes please!" Karla replied as she slipped into the bathroom. Karla and Young Boss laughed and made small talk as they watched cartoons. After breakfast, Karla showered and put her clothes back on from the night before minus her underwear. "Do you feel like closing your eyes again?" He asked. "If it's anything like the first part of our staycation, hell yeah!" She laughed as she dramatically squeezed her eyes shut and leaned towards him to put on a scarf. "Not yet silly." He laughed, he playfully slammed her on the bed and tickled her until she couldn't laugh anymore and then he kissed her as he looked into her eyes. "I'm serious this time, no bullshit, no other women, just me and you." He was so pressed to have her back because he hadn't met anyone like her, he just didn't realize it before. "I told you we'll see. You dogged me out the last time I gave you a chance but I do miss you a little bit." She playfully kissed him back and set up. They walked down the hallway, got on the elevator, walked down another long hallway and out of the double doors. He tied the bandanna around her head again, covering her eyes. He grabbed her hand and led her around the building to an open field with four stables of horses and removed the bandanna. "You've always wanted to go horseback riding, I remember everything" he said as he grabbed her hand. The smile on her face said it all, "oh my gosh" she trembled a bit, the idea was fun but the reality was sort of scary. "They're so big" she released a bit of nervousness as she gripped his hand tight. "You're riding with me right?" She asked. "What you tryna do break the horse's back? No!" He laughed and introduced her to the horse herder. "Which one do you want to ride young lady?" She heard him ask after telling her each of their names and a little about them. "Um, which one runs slow and likes beginners?" She nervously asked. "Conner is your horse, like I say, he's easy going, he can tell when you're nervous and he takes heed to that. Very gentle giant to say the least." He waved his hand for Karla to follow him. "Conner is beautiful!" She gazed at his nice dark brown coat and shiny black mane. "Here take pictures!" She threw her phone at Young Boss without thinking twice. She eased towards the horse and petted his face as he leaned a little low for her convenience. He batted his eyes slowly and smiled. "Oh my gosh, Conner just smiled at me! Did you get it?" She asked. In all the years he'd known Karla, Young Boss had never seen her so excited. "Yes baby, I got tons of pictures." He laughed. Seeing her this happy made him feel like a hero, he was doing a good job at making up for all his past fuckery. After thirty minutes of lessons, Karla was riding like a pro. Conner galloped across the open field gently enough to make her feel comfortable yet fast enough for her to truly enjoy her first horseback riding experience. The sun was shining, the breeze was perfect, Young Boss was snapping tons of pictures and Karla was having the time of her life.

"That was the best date I have ever been on in my entire life! I can't imagine it getting any better than that. What if we started seriously dating and you want to propose to me, how will you top that?" She asked jokingly as she leaned closer to the side and hugged his arm. "Oh that's only the beginning, just ride with me and this time don't leave. I mean that shit." Young Boss leaned closer towards her and kissed her forehead. She then remembered what the date was all about to begin with. "Just don't be into anything treacherous and we are good, I promise." She meant it from the bottom of her heart. He had won her back with the perfect date now she just had to prove to herself and her boss that he was a good guy.

Turned Leaf

"The marble floors give this place a nice accent, and the view is breathtaking! The kitchen is sort of small, but I love the stainless steel appliances and the marble countertops." Ja'Bria slowly inspected the 2 bedroom apartment in Buckhead. "They're asking for two-hundred and ten thousand for this spot. What do you think?" The realtor asked her. I should be buying with my brother, this is so shady. He can get paid and he'll probably negotiate for me. Ja'Bria thought as she was interrupted by her phone vibrating. "Oh, do you think they'll come down to one-hundred and seventy thousand?" She questioned, ready to leave and work with her brother. "I doubt it, they've already reduced the price by twenty-thousand". The realtor sounded aggravated. "I'll keep looking and get in touch with you in a week or so." She lied stuffing her home loan pre-approval letter in her Prada nap sack. "You're pre-approved for five-hundred thousand, what's the hold up?" The realtor asked becoming discouraged. It was the twelfth home he'd shown within a week and he still hadn't made any potential sells. "That doesn't mean I have it!" She lied. "Put in an offer for one-hundred and seventy thousand. Let me know what they say." She rolled her eyes and let herself out without waiting on the realtor. "Shit, I forgot I need a key card to get downstairs. I'll just stand here for a few minutes." She whispered to herself. Knock, knock, knock. "Are you coming?" Ja'Bria asked the agent, trying to play it off. "What, you forgot you can't get downstairs without the card?" He chuckled opening the door to invite her back in. "Um, I really need to go. I have an important test to study for." "Come in for a second and I'll let you go, just talk to me girl stop being so cold." He gave her a sincere smile and gently pulled her into the condo. "Loosen up, tell me what's bothering you." He questioned as he massaged her shoulders. Ja'Bria closed her eyes and enjoyed the massage. "I didn't realize my shoulders were so tight." She walked towards the balcony and relaxed. He followed still massaging her with the same rhythm. "Your attitude isn't far behind." He joked as he eased his hands away from her shoulders. "I know, I needed that. I just have so much going on right now. I mean trying to buy a place, finishing cosmetology school, breaking up with my boyfriend, drifting apart from my twin. My life isn't ideal right now." Anxiety shot through her body causing her to breathe faster than normal. "A yo shorty calm down, everybody goes through rough times. It will pass before you know it." He told her as he pulled two glasses from the cabinet and a bottle of Cabernet from the refrigerator. "Where did that come from?" She side eyed the realtor as he poured the wine. "I usually offer it to my clients if I think they'll enjoy a glass but your demeanor was fucked up so I didn't bother. Would you like some wine?" He joked as he handed her a glass. Bashfully, Ja'Bria looked down and accepted the glass. "I don't have anything special to do besides study, my test is five weeks away so I guess I can relax for a few minutes," she agreed. "What's on the test? I've never talked to someone in cosmetology school that I can remember. "There's sort of a chemistry section that I'm worried about. Certain hair products can't be mixed and others have to be mixed. Only certain hair types are compatible with certain hair chemicals and products. It's difficult. I'm also getting my nail technician license so I just have a lot going on." She opened up to him as she kneeled down to sit on the balcony's pavement. "Here this might help s little," he handed her a thin leather portfolio for her to sit on. "Thanks!" She smiled and scooted the portfolio under herself, he sat on the pavement along with her. "So how long have you been a real estate agent?" Ja'Bria asked. "For about six months, I used to own a barber shop but it wasn't doing too well. Haircuts were only twenty dollars at the most and the rent at the shop was eight thousand alone. I realized I was only breaking even or not even making the money to pay rent at all. My barbers couldn't come up with their booth rent so shit just got rough. I started off as an investor but I love real estate so I got my license. I'm not technically supposed to do both, but I have a few properties for sale too." The wine kicked in and before she knew it, Ja'Bria has leaned forward to kiss the realtor. *His lips are so smooth, his breath smells like mint, oh this cologne.* Ja'Bria caught herself a second too late. The realtor ran his hands through her silk wrap and pulled her onto his lap and caressed her smooth face. She raised her head for a breath of air and he kissed her neck leaving her no choice but to take it further. She gripped the top of his head admiring the neatly brushed waves and nibbled his ear as she worked her way to his neck; only five seconds passed before she felt him growing hard. "I... I have to go." She said as she jumped up and quickly fixed her clothes. He stood up, "I'm sorry, that was completely out of line but you started it." He smirked. "I know, I think the wine caught me off guard. It's been so long since..." Before she could finish her sentence he was kissing her again, leading her into the condo. "Seriously, I shouldn't." Ja'Bria declined before gathering her things and pulling him towards the door. "Girl you shouldn't have kissed me, I wanted you the moment I laid my eyes on you." The realtor leaned against the elevator wall and licked his lips as he sized her up. "I don't know what got into me, I'm so embarrassed... It's out of my character." She replied as she sashayed off the elevator and to her car. "Call me!" He refused to chase her through the garage but he wanted to get to know her better. *Damn she took her offer letter with her,*

I can't send her flowers or anything but I do have her phone number…

The person you are trying to reach does not answer, please leave a message or try your call again. "Bruh, I need to talk to you. Meet me at daddy's grave so we can talk." Ja'Bria said into the receiver as her knee trembled. To listen to your message dial one, to erase and re-record press two. "Nah, delete. Shit what should I say? How am I going to tell him? Ughhh!" She yelled as she deleted the message and hung up. "Bari whyyyy is your phone going straight to voicemail? Answer it!" She anxiously dialed him again, still no answer.

***

"What Omar, what, what, what!?" Ja'Bari answered after ignoring Omar's calls for the eighth time. "It's now or never, I got some paperwork that might change your life." Omar declared on the other end of the phone. Ja'Bari hesitated for a moment and slightly cocked his head to the side "It better be important and I don't want to hear any business proposals, no dry snitching, no bitch ass apologies and no crying about my sister leaving your sorry ass. Meet me at The Lounge in thirty minutes and don't plan to talk my head off. I have a business meeting at 4pm. Click." Ja'Bari didn't give Omar a chance to respond before he viciously hung up. I should shoot him in his damn skull, disrespectful bastard. Omar thought while speeding off into traffic. It was already 2:48 pm, that meant he was given all of fifteen minutes to show Ja'Bari what he'd discovered.

"Family or not, she's shading you man. Look at this shit." Overconfidently, Omar handed the papers over to Ja'Bari. "What is all of this? Big envelope, thick stack of papers, highlighted shit. What is all of this about Omar?" Ja'Bari quizzed. "I'd rather give you the pleasure or pain of reading it." "Yeah well wipe that slimed smile off of your dumb ass face before I do it for you." Ja'Bari rolled his eyes as he began reading. Contingent distributions: $1,300,000 to be evenly divided between Ja'Bria Elise White and Ja'Bari beneficiaries listed in paragraph A. Ja'Bari Ellis White, Ja'Bria Elise White. "Why you always gotta be disrespectful Bari? We were so much better than that." "Man shut the fuck up I'm trying to read besides how did you get this, don't you know it's illegal to go through someone's mail? It's a federal offense." Ja'Bari showed no emotion, not giving in to Omar's eager revenge plot. "It came in the mail. I've been trying to get in touch with Ja'Bria but she won't answer. She left all of her clothes here, she has piles of mail at the house and everything. "I don't blame her, but why are you opening her mail?" Ja'Bari was skeptical of everything that was going on. "How do I know this is even real? I ain't never seen a will." "I would be a sick bastard to make this up Ja'Bari, I'm just looking out for my partner." "Your fifteen minutes are up; I have a business meeting to go to and don't ever refer to me as your god-damned partner again." Ja'Bari snatched the papers, shoved them into the envelope and stormed out of the bar. He can't hide the fact that he's pissed off, I hope he kills that bitch. I don't give a fuck if he is her brother. She wanna come up on some money and not tell me? Fucking leave me when she gets on? I'll see to it that Ja'Bari is on my side and I'll eventually convince him to share the wealth... A grimy smile spread across Omar's face as he was stopped in mid thought by the waitress. "Is everything okay, do you want to order?" "Oh nah I'm good, I'm about to get up out of here. Got some work to do."

Goodness Gracious

"I got half way out of the garage and my car slowed down and stopped." Karla said into the receiver as she walked back into the town home she practically shared with Young Boss. "Okay ma'am, it'll be about 2 hours before a tow truck will make it, there's traffic- is that alright?" "I'm supposed to be at work by ten o' clock, no that's not okay." Karla hit the speaker phone button as she texted Ja'Bari. *Car problems, I'm going to be late. I'm so sorry! Be there as soon as I can!* "Come on, let me push it out of the garage," Young Boss slid his timberland boots on and rushed down the stairs. "I'll just call you all back, I hope traffic dies down." Karla hung up the phone and threw it in her cup hole. "Put it in neutral bae," Young Boss said as he positioned himself behind the car to push it. "There we go, straighten your wheel and put it back in park." "Thank you baby. Ahhh my car is basically new, what's wrong with it?" "It's probably your timing belt or something like that. It's all good, I'll take you to work and have your car fixed by the time you get off," Young Boss promised as he walked over to his car. "No that's okay, I'll wait to get my car towed." Karla hesitated. "Girl come on!" He said smiling. Anxiety rushed her body as she slowly got into the car. "Why you look like you saw a ghost? The hell you got going on?" "My car just broke down on me, why I gotta have something going on!?" "That's life baby girl, I got you. Damn, I ain't never been to your job that's crazy. What's the address?" "Umm, I don't even know the exact address. Let's just play hooky, I'm already late!" "You're already dressed too!" He laughed entering the highway. "Get off on 32nd and I'll direct you there." "Ain't no Porsche dealership over there." "I said I work at a dealership that primarily sells Porsches. Turn right here and a left at the path mart." "Oh hell no! This is the dealership Ja'Bari owns!? Wow, small world. I'm turning around." "Why? How do you know my boss?" Karla acted totally clueless. "Remember when I told you I don't know who I can trust? That's who set me up..." "Why did you whip into the gas station like that!? You almost made me catch whiplash!" Karla rolled her eyes. "You can work at that trifling ass dealership or you can be my girl, you make the choice but I'm not taking you there." "Wait, what happened? I don't think Ja'Bari is trifling at all, there must be a misunderstanding." Karla shook her head. "He put drugs in the trunk of the car I rented from him for a video. The case is still under investigation but he's a shady motherfucker. Everybody ain't a hater but from what I hear, Ja'Bari is and ain't no room for his kind in my circle of affiliates." Young Boss was furious. "How do I know you ain't trying to help that clown frame me? I mean you don't owe me no loyalty, hell you work for him." He raced through traffic trying to shake off the possible betrayal. "Slow down! First of all, where did you hear this from? Why do you think Ja'Bari set you up? That man has businesses to run and he ain't really tying to mess it up, he supports young people with ambition and honestly I could see him admiring your hustle. Look, he has millions and he's not looking to stop anyone from making their own. Why don't you re-evaluate your circle a little closer?" "Man Omar told me all about Ja'Bari. He's a bitter dude who hates on everybody who's doing something. He ain't got it like you think and he definitely set me up. Who else would have had time to put all that stuff in the trunk? Who would have thought to do it huh? Tell me that and you might help him save face but I ain't got no mercy on him. I slick wanna bash his face in." "I'm not sure but I highly doubt he'd want to put everything he's worked so hard for in jeopardy." "What are you sleeping with him or something, how do you know what he's capable of!?" "You need to calm down, what kind of person do you think I am? Wow…" "You seem to…"

"Shh! Hello?" "Hey Karla where you at? Is everything okay with the car?" Ja'Bari asked. "Yes, I'm getting it towed. Hey are you busy right now?" "Not right now but I do need you to come to the office if you can, got some paperwork that needs to be filed and I have a few contracts we're signing this evening." "Okay, I'll be there in a few. Do you have a few minutes to spare? I have someone I want you to meet with." "I have about fifteen minutes to spare, see you soon!" Ja'Bari hung up and paced the floor for a moment. *I don't know whether I'm coming or going, Lord help me.* He sat in his office chair, kicked his feet up on the window seal and lit his cigar.

"Hey Ja'Bari! Boss is out there and I think it's time that you two have a conversation. I think I know what's going on a little bit but I'll let you be the judge of that." "I really don't feel like dealing with that shit, I don't know if I can deal with anymore right now." Ja'Bari ran his hands across his smooth waved hair and sternly looked at Karla, "send him in." Karla swiftly twisted through the office. Finally she could prove her boyfriend's innocence. "Follow me bae, I think both of you will enjoy what each other has to say." "It better be good, I'm in this man's dwelling and I don't even trust him. Straight bullshit." "Dwelling?" Karla laughed at Young Boss' choice of words. "I just want you two to figure out the entire truth, it may keep you out of trouble too!" She knocked on Ja'Bari's glass window and he motioned for her to come in. "Ja'Bari this is Young Boss, Boss this is Ja'Bari. Not sure if you two have met directly but be honest, don't hold anything back and please you two get to the bottom of things." She pressed her hands together as if she were praying for them. "Let us talk in private bae." Young Boss said as he stood at the door. "Come in son, sit down." Ja'Bari insisted. "First, let me ask you this; why did you always give Omar an excuse to not pay in full to rent my cars and homes? Do you realize how much money you owe us?" Boss paused and rubbed his chin for a second before responding *I don't owe him shit! How can I put this without being so blunt?* "How much was I supposed to be paying? As far as I knew, twelve thousand took care of everything. If not, my apologies. I'll pay you what I owe you, maybe Omar wasn't clear. He never told me I owed him anything." Anger rushed through Ja'Bari, *stay calm and hear lil dude out. He might not be lying but somebody is and they will pay. Breathe Ja'Bari just breathe...* "Enough of the small talk, how much do I owe you? I'll bring it back this evening or you can meet me somewhere." "Omar shot three of your videos, right?" Ja'Bari asked as he stroked his chin. "Yeah three videos, the last one turned into a catastrophe. I can't believe you were sloppy enough to put that heavy weight in the trunk of an exotic whip like that." Young Boss said as his nostrils flared from annoyance. "Hold up, I ain't never been sloppy and I got too much to lose to even fuck with the streets. What you got a fucking wire on, you trying to set me up in my own shit?" Ja'Bari's voice became aggressive and higher than before. "Man hell no I don't have a wire on. If it wasn't yours, whose was it?" Young Boss twisted his mouth sideways. "I thought you were coming here to apologize for being sloppy in my car. We'll get around to that but first back to this money that you paid Omar. Exactly how much did you pay him per video?" "Twelve thousand even the first two times, six thousand the second time because we didn't finish after the whole drug bust." Young Boss gritted his teeth and grilled Ja'Bari. "Look lil dude, I don't care who you are in these streets, on the radio or to your momma. Keep grillin' me like that and it's gon be a problem. Now for the last time, I didn't put the drugs there but I think we're getting somewhere." Ja'Bari slid both palms down the sides of his face. "You gave him twelve bands the first two times, right?" "Yeah I did, why?" "He told me you gave him six thousand so who should I believe? I don't know you from a can of paint." Ja'Bari stated. "Check my resume big homie, I'm pretty reputable. You seem to be too. We should really be checking out this Omar guy. What do you know about him?" Young Boss asked staring Ja'Bari in the face and raising his eyebrow. Ja'Bari paused before answering, *he might be right hell; I don't know much about Omar other than he's my sister's boyfriend. That's none of his business though, shit could go left real quick if Omar has been shady. What if this little dude is playing me and he's the one I need to watch? He does have a valid point, I've never heard anything bad about him I just don't like all the flexing, that is a part of his job though.* "Look man," Young Boss interrupted Ja'Bari's thoughts, I'm not going out of my way to convince you of anything, everything done in the dark comes to light. This Omar cat is no good, word to the wise, watch him, hell I know I will." "Oh trust me, I'm watching everything and everyone. Nobody gets a pass." There was a sense of relief that Young Boss had told Ja'Bari everything he needed to know at the moment. "Here's my card and let me write my personal cell number on the back, not too many people have it, feel free to hit me whenever you need to. We'll work it out." Ja'Bari assured the young rapper. "Alright boss, I will be in touch I need to get back to this hustle so I can live like you one day." Young Boss said. Remarks like that didn't always sit well with Ja'Bari, it could be taken as a forewarning to a robbery but for some reason he saw it as admiration. *If he had said he wanted what I have, shit could've gone left quick.* Ja'Bari smirked at his own ruthless mentality. "Hell you smiling at man?" Young Boss laughed as he walked out of the office. "You got a bright future ahead of you man." Ja'Bari chuckled. "Be easy man and take care, let's do lunch next week sometime." "Alright, I'll have your secretary set it up" Young Boss said as they both burst into laughter.

G Code Chronicles

After squaring away paper work for the new studio Young Boss decided to purchase, he struck a conversation. "I need a house too boss, can we find something in the cut? Something far enough from the city to be ducked off but close enough to still claim the set?" Ja'Bari and Young Boss laughed. "Of course we can, but may I ask where in the hell you're getting all of this money?" Ja'Bari was curious. The rap game is a joke to some people and the money isn't that good unless you strike platinum which is one in one-thousand. "I've been saving up, I paid off this town home I got and everything I used to spend on my mortgage is in an account. I've invested in a few side projects I believed in. The return on my investment was sweeter than I expected." Young Boss smirked proud of his accomplishments. "Word. I can dig it young boss." Ja'Bari motioned a salute and stood up. "Take a look at some of the houses I pulled and tell me what you think." Ja'Bari added offering his seat. "Damn all of this for less than a half a million!?" Young Boss' mouth and eyes were wide open. "Run it!" He added turning the computer screen around. "They're asking four-hundred and seventy-five thousand. What's your offer?" Ja'Bari scanned through the pictures. "Offer three-hundred fifty thousand." *Your dream home for a fraction of the cost! This six bedroom, four and a half bathroom mini-mansion boasts a gourmet kitchen with new stainless steel appliances, an island for preparing and or serving food, a breakfast bar and an open area for dining. The oversized open living room has floor to ceiling Windows, hardwood floors and an electric fireplace with real fire! The master bathroom has a double vanity and jacuzzi tub with a separate shower. The backyard is perfect for gatherings or relaxing, there's a nice sized swimming pool, three gazebos all on three acres of land. This won't last long, call us to view this beautiful home today!*

Young Boss drifted off into a daydream of a gangsta party by the pool. "I can see it now, fine ass girls in bikini's, steak, shrimp, lobster and crab legs cooking on the grill, champagne flowing everywhere and all my people enjoying life." He said leaning back in Ja'Bari's seat. "Get yo ass up!" Ja'Bari laughed. "I'll put in the offer. Take a look at a few more houses on the list though just in case." He said nodding towards the computer screen. "Ah, yes. I'm calling about the home you have listed at 2132 Brickenbridge Lane. I have a client who's interested in viewing the home." Ja'Bari said into the receiver. "Oh, I've just received an offer on this home but I'll keep your information and follow up with you if something doesn't go through." The agent replied. "Absolutely, I believe we've worked together before. I'm Ja'Bari, lock me in." "Oh yes, yes. Ja'Bari, I remember. I have your number here and I'll definitely follow up with you. Nice talking to you again." "Yes, you too. Don't be a stranger, my client is offering cash." Ja'Bari added before hanging up. "What? What did he say?" "Someone put in an offer, keep looking but don't let that get you down." "What about those houses you have listed? The ones you used to let me shoot videos in?" "I have about eighteen houses listed right now, they're all listed at over one million dollars. What's your budget?" "Under five-hundred thousand if possible. That way I can pay cash, I hate financing things." "You've rightfully earned that stage name of yours. That's some real boss shit lil homie." Ja'Bari was impressed, he liked kicking it with Young Boss. Off the record, he was mature and he proved time and time again that he was worthy of a particular status.

"Bae, I really want these shoes at Saks. They're holding my size." Karla cooed on the other end of the phone. "Aight, how much are they?" Young boss asked, wondering if he should tell her where the stash was. "Two g's… I know that's a lot but that can be my birthday, Christmas and Valentine's Day present." She said nearly crossing her fingers. "Aight man, I'll be home in bout' two hours." He hung up the phone to keep her wondering. If she called again or texted still talking about those shoes she wasn't getting anything. "Karla be working my damn nerves, I'm trying to buy her a house and she askin' for shoes and shit." Young Boss said proudly. He was happy to have a spoiled ass girlfriend but he got irritated when she called while he was handling business. "Shut up, you love that shit." Ja'Bari chuckled, he knew the feeling. "Aye, they only want two-hundred twenty five thousand for this!? What's wrong with it?" Young Boss got excited all over again. "Oh, this shit is real playa like." Ja'Bari browsed through the pictures. "Nothing is wrong with it, they had a lean on the house and they owe the back pay on the HOA fees so they're asking twenty thousand up front. Oh, the price is firm too" Ja'Bari confirmed. "Word! Can we go look at it now?" Young Boss was ecstatic, the house had five bedrooms, three and a half bathrooms, not to mention the master bedroom had high cathedral ceilings and boasted a large balcony. "Let's take separate cars, gotta stop by the mall when we leave." They both gathered their belongings and headed out.

"The lock box won't budge" Ja'Bari said, aligning the box with his iPhone and tugging. After the third attempt, he searched in his phone by the address and realized he had a new email.

Ja'Bari,

We're taking it off the market, we've negotiated a payoff amount with the bank. We saved our house! We'll be moving back in on the 15th of next month. Thank you for everything, you can remove the listing.

Regards,

Mr. And Mrs. Brown

"Damnit man! We just wasted our time. Don't get discouraged tho', we can look at more houses. The seller backed out, they saved their house." Ja'Bari explained as Young Boss looked at him with a blank expression. *Does this motherfucker really know what he's doing? That's the second house that flopped. My patience is wearing thin but I heard buying a house was one of the most frustrating things to do.* Young Boss thought to himself as he scrolled through his Instagram timeline. "Aight man, I'm on my way to the mall." He said stashing his phone in his back pocket. "Me too man, I need to pick Tatiana up a gift or two. I haven't spent time with her in weeks." Ja'Bari brushed his forehead disappointed in himself. "Yeah man, take care of home. What are you going to get her?" "Probably some perfume, a dress and some shoes. Tell her to get dressed." "Oh that's smooth, take her to the Polo Bar. I'll have my manager make reservations for you, it's hard to get into that place but the experience is worth it." Young Boss offered. "Appreciate it man, try for 9:30 reservations." Ja'Bari said as they hopped in separate cars.

"Oh yeah, you can't go wrong with the black dress. These are the shoes Karla begged for, they are dope." Young Boss smirked. "Yeah those are fresh, help me find some shoes to go with this dress." Ja'Bari said holding the dress up to himself as if it were his. They both laughed and walked towards the shoes. "These go hard" Ja'Bari admired a pair of black six inch Jimmy Choo sling back pumps. "Yes, very fucking classy." Young Boss said in a dramatic tone.

Don't Think About It..

"Honestly, I think he's getting tired of me anyway. The flame has burned out." Tatiana said into the receiver. "I'm pretty sure he's cheating. He was looking at every woman that walked by in Turks and Caicos. Fuck him Sis, you deserve better. Trust me, Ja'Bari isn't the man he claims he is." Omar smirked, he was getting somewhere. "He has all of that money and doesn't use it to spend time with you? Get the fuck out of here," he continued. "He used to but he seems distant now. Ain't that your homeboy tho? Why are you dissin' him behind his back?" Tatiana questioned as she peeped through the blinds. "I'm just keepin' it real with you. You my sister and I know you can do better than that." "I'm your sister because my boyfriend and your ex-girlfriend are brother and sister not for any other reason so why should I trust you? How do I know you're not just bitter because Ja'Bria left you?" Tatiana spat back annoyed. "The proof is in the pudding sis, he comes home late, y'all don't do anything extra anymore, he's definitely seeing other girls. I mean really, why hasn't he proposed to you yet or at least planned on it?" Omar was trying to hit a sensitive subject but Tatiana didn't buy it. "Look, at the end of the day our relationship has nothing to do with you. I don't even know why you called me…"

"I didn't want to have to do this, but Ja'Bari has another girlfriend and he's getting pretty serious with her." Omar lied. "Whatever Omar, get off my damn line!" Tatiana hung up the phone frazzled. She didn't know what to believe, she only knew how she felt and she was feeling neglected. Tears streamed down her face as she drifted off into a nap. "Why would you do this to me? I've stood by your side, cooked your dinner, washed your clothes or took them to the cleaners, cleaned up for you, promised to never leave your side. Why!?" "Baby calm down, it's not what it looks like. This is my sister, just please baby, put your shoes back on and come here." "Get off of me!" Tatiana whimpered in her sleep as Ja'Bari slightly shook her to wake her up. "Wake up baby." He leaned forward and whispered in her ear. She opened her eyes and looked foolishly before realizing it was just a dream. I got something for him, two can play this game... Tatiana thought as she snatched away from him. "Are you alright?" He raised his eyebrow as he stood up. "I'm fine, just know what's done in the dark always comes to light." She sassed sliding to the edge of the bed. "I know that's right" Ja'Bari laughed. He didn't know what kind of dream she had but he could certainly agree with what she was saying. "Close your eyes." He smiled. Tatiana's heart warmed up as she smiled back, "okay!" She closed her eyes tight and held out her left hand. For a moment he felt bad, realizing that she was ready for marriage. He slid the smaller shopping bag around her wrist and sat the larger one at her feet. "Open." He said as he stood over her to see if she liked the gifts. "Get dressed, we have dinner at nine." "Aww, thanks boo." She said as she pulled the classic Marc Jacobs dress out of the bag and held it against her chest. "Okay, okay" she added to assure her satisfied opinion. "These are bomb as hell, who helped you pick them out and what's the occasion?" She asked, shooting him a suspicious look. "Nothing baby, it's just that I've been so busy that I haven't made time for my special lady. I want you to know how important you are to me." He confessed. Confused and pleased, Tatiana slightly let down her guard and began getting ready. *Maybe I just don't keep myself up anymore, my hair is a mess, I've almost forgotten how to do my makeup and my nails haven't been done in three weeks!* She thought to herself as she grabbed the nail polish remover from under the sink. "Hurry up, it's 5:45 already and I know you have a lot to do." Ja'Bari called from the other side of the bathroom door. "I'll be out of the shower in thirty minutes!" Tatiana yelled as she quickly rubbed the old nail polish off her nails. She tied her hair with a scarf and turned on the shower as she connected her cell phone to the bluetooth speaker that sat on the sink. "Cruisin' down the west side high waaaay, doin' things I like to do my waaaay." She sang Beyonce and Jay-Z's old hit 'Bonnie and Clyde' to the top of her lungs as she lathered her body with soap. "You can't sing" Ja'Bari said sliding the glass door and joining Tatiana. "Get out!" She giggled, splashing soap suds on his chest. "Come here" he demanded as he pulled her close and planted his soft lips against hers. He kissed her softly and caressed the small of her back until she was fully relaxed. "Baby I'm sorry I've been neglecting you" he whispered in her ear before proceeding to make love to her. That nearly turned Tatiana off because she felt like he was acting guilty but she didn't refuse, she lifelessly gave in and let him continue.

"What's up with you?" He asked as they got dressed. Tatiana filed her nails and scowled at him before she uttered a word. "Why are you acting so got damned guilty Ja'Bari? What are you hiding?" She questioned, deciding against revealing what she'd heard. "Nothing bae, why I gotta be hiding something because I've been working hard?" He asked in an aggravated tone. Tears streamed down her face as Omar's voice replayed in her head, *Ja'Bari ain't the dude he claims to be...* "Shit! I'm over here spilling nail polish all on my comforter. Just leave me alone!" She cried as she closed the bottle of polish and snatched the comforter off the bed. "Are you pms'ing or something? What in the hell is wrong with you?" He asked as he towered over her slightly pissed. "I've been breaking my back for us to live good and all you can do is cry and act a fool because I've been putting in work?" Tatiana didn't flinch, instead she just made the decision to do things on her own terms. "Ja'Bari get the fuck out of my face right now." She calmly demanded. "Whatever, finish getting dressed. They'll charge my card if we don't show."

"Party of two for 9:30? Right this way." A hostess dresses in what seemed to be a tailored Ralph Lauren suit directed them. The restaurant was dimly lit and filled with many people of importance. "This is very nice Ja'Bari, what made you bring me here? How did you even get reservations? I heard there's a thirty day wait list and ten minutes after they start taking reservations, it's closed." Tatiana rambled as she gazed at the surroundings. "You know I'm plugged in everywhere in one way or another." He boasted as he scanned the menu. "So tell me, are you doing this to make up for cheating on me or you about to propose?" she asked getting straight to her concerns. Ja'Bari took a big gulp of ice cold water before responding. "Neither one" he replied nonchalantly as he pretended he didn't know what he would order. "Stop looking at that damned menu and look at me." Tatiana firmly demanded. "Look, I'm tired of trying to explain myself and prove to you that I'm not cheating. Fuck it, believe what you want but don't mess up my dinner, this is my first time eating here" he scowled. "Can't wait to meet a grateful girl, man damn!" He grunted under his breath. "I heard you! So what, is your new girlfriend just as ungrateful as me!?" She threw her balled up napkin across the table and stormed off. Ja'Bari leaned back and tried to act unfazed. He wasn't going to attract any ignorant ass attention and he wasn't going to chase her crazy ass.

"What the hell is wrong with you and where did you go?" Ja'Bari asked in a low but firm tone. Tatiana looked at her phone for a moment before responding. "I needed some fresh air" she said after contemplating getting an über back home. "Get yo crazy ass back in here, the waitress is waiting on you." He grunted and hung up. Tatiana raised her eyebrow, *I'll go back in there when the fuck I please. Who does he think he is?* She sat on the bench outside of the restaurant twirling her hair and waiting for him to beg her to come back. Ja'Bari looked at his phone, glanced at the door, looked at his phone again and informed the waitress he'd be right back. "Tatiana…" She jumped as he startled her, she was going through a dude on Instagram's pictures. "Is that why you're acting crazy? You've been talking to this clown and you think I'm doing the same thing, right?" He huffed, snatching the phone from Tatiana's hand. "Ja'Bari fuck you." She sucked her teeth and rolled her eyes as she strutted back into the five star restaurant. "Nah, fuck you with yo sneaky ass." He retorted as he followed behind her. He knew she wasn't talking to the dude on Instagram by the way she answered but he still didn't know where her insecurities were coming from. *I mean yeah, I have been working hard but that's because I wanna stack enough to get a nice ring and have a beautiful wedding without it fazing me. A ring gon' cost almost twenty stacks alone, I heard weddings are about forty grand…* "what the fuck you sittin' there lookin' all confused for?" Tatiana spat as she glared up from looking at the menu. "I'm just trying to figure out when you started cheating on me" he lied. "You can hang that tired ass lie up, ain't nobody got time to be cheating." She rolled her eyes. "So why do you think I do? Hell I'm the one out here busting my ass stacking check after check so you can blow money…" She contemplated revealing her sources once more before blurting out, "I heard you were cheating on me, if there's something I'm not doing right or if I'm not enough for you, just let me know Ja'Bari. What can I do to make it better?" She lowered her head feeling less of a woman. "You heard?" He paused and decided not to dig too deep at dinner. "Like I said, I don't have time to think about cheating. Truth be told, I'm working my ass off so we can build. It would be nice if you worked more and helped a little around the house. Buy the groceries or something. That's all I'd ask for if you're comfortable with that, but there's definitely not another woman in the picture." *Damn, because I don't buy groceries he's tired of me? Why didn't he just say something? I'm going to work hard, stack my money and dip on him. I'm tired of his ungrateful ass…* Tatiana just smirked. "Fine, I'll do whatever I gotta do."

"Thank you for the dress and shoes, the perfume smells amazing too." Tatiana broke the silence and forced a smile. "Yeah... You're welcome." Ja'Bari switched lanes. The rain was pouring rapidly, Tatiana leaned her head against the window and dozed off. Ja'Bari glanced over at her as he stopped at the intersection. *Why am I still with her, she does seem to only be around for convenience. She's well kept, hardly works, and does what she wants to do all day. Even if I was cheating, who is she to address it? Ugh. Do I really want her to be the mother of my children? My wife? She's stagnant. Ain't nothing to her but a pretty face and a sweet personality. That shit can only go so far. If I fell, she'd fall too. That'll never happen though...* Ja'Bari smiled and brushed his chin as he cruised into the garage. He didn't know his next move but the relationship between he and Tatiana was getting old. *She's a rider as far as I know but she ain't got shit to offer me for real. I deserve a bossed up girl that I can grow with.* His thoughts lingered as he flung open the door to the house. Tatiana continued mentally mapping out her plan to move on.

Cutting the Grass

"You know the one thing I didn't do was find out who used to own this studio before I bought it." Young Boss said into the receiver. "Yeah, I was so hell bent on you investing in your dreams before you changed your mind that I didn't really ask either. Plus the deal was amazing." Ja'Bari had to admit. "I'm over here cleaning up, tryna get ready for this grand opening and look at what I found…" Young Boss said as he sent Ja'Bari a picture of a wall full of bullet holes. "Where the hell was that!?" Ja'Bari wracked his brain trying to remember if he'd heard of any industry beef lately. "Behind that big ghetto ass picture of Biggie, Pac, Aaliyah, Lefteye…" "Ohhh, by the vending machine?" Ja'Bari interrupted. "Man, hell yeah." Young Boss interjected. They both paused for a moment wondering who, when and why. "I was trying to get it fixed up before I surprised everyone with the new studio but I gotta make some phone calls so I won't get caught up in the beef. Find out who was shooting and get the message out that their target is long gone." Young Boss assured. "Aight bet, if I find out anything about it I'll definitely let you know." Ja'Bari assured Young Boss before hanging up.

Tatiana unzipped and stepped out of her dress,

slipped into her white cozy house robe, slid her bedroom slippers on and skipped down the stairs. *I can show him better than I can tell him.* She thought right before slipping down the last few steps and banging her head. "Ooouuuccchhh!" She yelled in slow motion. Ja'Bari did everything he could to keep from laughing once he realized she was okay. "Get up, sit on the couch, I'll get you an ice pack" he said with little to no empathy. She crawled onto the couch and massaged the back of her head with one hand and grabbing her iPad with the other. "Here" Ja'Bari handed her the ice pack and headed upstairs. *Damn, she couldn't pick up the dress off the floor?* He thought as he stepped over it. Ja'Bari undressed, threw his clothes into the dirty clothes basket, stepped into a pair of baseball shorts and relaxed in the center of his California King. "Get em' LeBron!" he yelled at the television. ESPN was the only thing on his mind until he dozed off.

Meanwhile, Tatiana scrolled through a few condos and made a mental note of the monthly rents. *Hmmm, what kind of long term job do I want? I know a secretary ain't much to some, but I actually like the work. I'm organized as hell...* She pulled her laptop out of the couch console and updated her resume.

The Business

"Ahh man stop playing." Ja'Bari sighed after following up with his fellow realtor. "Yeah man some beef about money so I hear, but he was ready to get a bigger studio anyway. He and his wife just bought a nice crib in another area, he wanted to be closer to home, they've started having a family." "Who was the video production crew, do you know?" Ja'Bari had the strangest feeling in the pit of his stomach. "Nah, I just know he shot a few rounds and dipped. He didn't even hit anyone, they said he was a nervous wreck." The realtor concluded. "Alright thank you man, I'll holla at you later." Ja'Bari ended the call and immediately called Young Boss. "Have you heard anything?" "Man it was Omar's punk ass shooting at somebody's manager!" Young Boss said as he paced back and forth. "He probably knows the ins and outs of the building man" he added. "Ugh, that explains the feeling I had when I was talking to the realtor. It used to be Maze's studio but that's not who the beef was with," Ja'Bari said as he placed the phone on speaker and palmed his face. "And fuck Omar, he ain't gon do shit" he added trying to comfort Young Boss. "Man I don't want the cat around me and knowing what I do... How long do I have to change my mind?" Young Boss was irritated. "You got two weeks in all so you probably have about three days now. Just know you might not get another studio with the equipment included... Besides, I know you ain't gon let O chump you out of your dream. He probably won't step foot near that place. Besides, he'll get ran out of the city soon. This is our city!" Ja'Bari rambled, hoping Young Boss would find motivation to keep the studio. Young Boss paused and looked up at the ceiling, looked around the fully furnished and equipped studio and smiled. "Yeah you know what, you're right. Fuck Omar." He chuckled for a moment. "I wish he would try something stupid." He added as he continued cleaning up and rearranging things. "At least we know a little more about him now. Anyway, enough about lil dude, I'm thinking about having the grand opening next Saturday" Young boss said enthusiastically. "That's what I'm talking about. What do you need for me to do?" "Invite some high-sidity broads." They shared a laugh. "Alright man, what else?" "Any hood rich clientele that you may have, I need to expand my network. Man, I'm thinking about signing artists pretty soon. I need to retire from the rap game in about ten years." Ja'Bari let out a burst of laughter again. "What man, I'm serious." "I'll invite a few people I know, we can definitely turn it into a networking event. This way, people will know where to start if they need a network for anything." "True, sometimes I want to keep the studio low-key and other times I want it to be bunkin' all day. You feel me?" "Of course I do. Just remember, the more traffic, the bigger the risk but the bigger the risk, the larger the profit." Ja'Bari advised Young Boss before they ended the conversation.

Blood is Always...

"Bari!!! What's up? What's been going on with you? I haven't heard from you in ages!" Ja'Bria said ecstatically. "Getting a few things together. I want you and a few of the fly girls you kick it with to come to my boys grand opening at his new studio." "Word, when? Some bosses gon' be there?" She asked, finally ready to hit the scene again as a sane single lady. "Of course, but don't pick up any stray dogs without running them by me first." Ja'Bari laughed, her taste in men was bad from what he'd seen. "Oh hush, everybody is a fool once or twice in their life. When is it?" "Next weekend, dress to impress, red carpet event, networking and more. You should probably bring your lil iPad mini, you'll make a few contacts I'm sure." He told her as he looked at his other phone. "How's graduation going anyway? Do you need anything?" Ja'Bari asked his sister. "Nope, just a bomb ass graduation gift! Oh, I've been meaning to tell you..." she started, "Sis, hold that thought. I'll call you back in fifteen minutes." Ja'Bari said before hanging up. It was a broker that he was working with to close on a million dollar house. "It's a go, now let's get this money homie." Chris, the realtor said as he pounded his fist on his desk in excitement. Ja'Bari smiled, "let's get it," he agreed before hanging up. His adrenaline rushed as he zipped through traffic bumpin' Jeezy, *bitch I'm amazin', look what I'm blazin', eyes so low that I look like an Asian, forever clubbin', forever thuggin', then haters run they mouth, they ain't talkin' bout nothin'…* he was amped as he pulled into his dealership. *Man, look at this. I did all of this with my willpower and my team. I'm living out my dreams. Thank you Lord, I'm extremely blessed and I won't take it for granite.* He gave thanks before stepping out of his E-Class Mercedes Benz.

"Boss, guess what?" Karla said as she greeted him at the door. "Move girl you're crowding my space, what?" He said playfully pushing her to the side. "Haha whatever! We sold all three of the Lamborghini's yesterday. Three Indian's came in and dropped straight cash!" She twirled around and rushed to her desk. "Here's the sales sheet, look!" Jabari's eyes bulged as he reviewed the documents. "They didn't finance them?" He asked in excitement. "Nope" she smiled with confidence as she sat at her desk and kicked her feet up. She watched Ja'Bari review the sales over and over in amazement. "Keep doing the right thing and you'll continue to be blessed." Karla added as she continued filing digital paperwork. "Wait, who sold these cars? Sean, the new dude?" Ja'Bari asked. "Yes, I helped him with all of the paperwork but he sold them" she confirmed. Ja'Bari rushed into his office to check his emails and to review the quarterly sales report. One point five million in revenue? I must be dreaming…

He gazed out of his office window expecting to wake up at any moment but it never happened, he was in fact receiving blessings on top of blessings. The first thing he did was review his payroll. He handles Human Resources although he needed someone else to do the job. Karla kept things in order like no other and she seemed to be content. There was no better time to give her a promotion and a hefty pay raise. He went into the payroll system and changed her annual salary from $27,000 to $32,000.

Greetings Karla,

I would like to take a moment to congratulate you on a job well done, and to offer you a new position as we shift into the third quarter of the fiscal year.

If you accept, I would like to offer you the position as the new Human Resources Coordinator. I've briefly reviewed your resume and I see that you have a Bachelor's Degree in Human Resources.

Please step into my office for a short interview once you've received this email.

Best Regards,

Ja'Bari Smith
CEO/Owner

Smith Luxury Automobiles

Ja'Bari smiled as he continued to add quarterly bonuses and increase salaries. *It's time to take it a notch higher…*

"Are you serious or is this some type of cruel April Fools Joke!?" Karla barged into his office. "You need to learn how to knock, you scared the shit out of me!" Ja'Bari jumped, grabbing the corner of his desk. "Have a seat" he instructed her as he gathered his thoughts. "You graduated two weeks ago, right?" He asked remembering the vacation days she had taken. "Yes! I graduated from CAU!" She exclaimed. "Great, what do you know about HR?" "Well, I did HR in the admissions office, it was considered work study but I learned how to set up payroll, I learned a lot about workers' comp, PTO, background checks, interviewing…" "Alright, alright, I got you. You seem like you know enough to accept the offer." "Yes Ja'Bari, I'd love to take you up on the offer. When do I start?" "Thirty minutes ago." He had the silliest smirk on his face as they burst into laughter. "How did you know I'd say yeah?" "Because you're loyal." Ja'Bari slightly raised his head to look at her expression. "You are too man, I could probably go somewhere else and make more money but you allow flexible hours, bonuses, a comfortable yet professional environment… I could go on for days but I really do appreciate you. You're like a boss ass big brother." She giggled as she hopped out of her chair and gave him a big bear hug."Awww man get off of me and go do some work. As a matter of fact, follow me." He led her towards her new office. "This office used to be mine before they did a little reconstruction in here. Here's your key too. Let me get some of the fellas in here to move your computer." Ja'Bari reached in his pocket for the key to Karla's new office. Her face lit up like a light bulb. "All of this for me!?" she asked as she spun around and gazed at her new desk. "Yes boss lady, get to it. Start moving your little fashion magazines and nail files. Hopefully you'll have some real work to do soon." He laughed as he walked out and gave her time to enjoy her new office before her things were moved.

TRAPPED

Tatiana sat in the center of the bed as she stared at the oversized basket of laundry. *See, he won't even acknowledge the fact that I wash his dirty drawers, cook delicious meals and work from time to time.* She chuckled, knowing that was her downfall.

That's it! I'll start working and stop doing things around the house. She smirked in hopes of proving a point. "Let's go to the Grand Opening of Young Boss' new studio tonight!" Her homegirl called interrupting her thoughts. "I don't have anything to wear girl. What are you wearing?" "Go get something! Girl you need to get out of the house anyway, didn't you say that you and Bari have been going through it? Let's have a ladies' night." Her friend pressed. "Okay girl, well let me get started early. You know how the hair salon can be." Tatiana hopped in the shower and threw on a VS PINK jogging suit and a pair of Nike flip flops. As she pulled out of the driveway in her charcoal 328i, she noticed a F150 backed into the cul da sac. Distracted, she drove off without closing the garage door. As she fixed her eyes on the rearview mirror, she missed Ja'Bari as he zoomed past her.

Damnit! I was almost in there and Tatiana's ditsy ass left the garage door opened. Fuck it, I'll confront

Ja'Bria at the grand opening tonight... Omar's thoughts raced as he tried to figure out how to track Ja'Bria down. It literally drove him crazy that she had completely cut him off and her brother cutting all ties only made matters worse. His heart pounded as he tried to drive normally out of the neighborhood. "Shit!" He squealed as he stepped on the gas. He saw a light flick on in Ja'Bari's house as Omar pulled into the drive through at Popeyes. "Helloooo? May I take your order?" The cashier emphasized over the intercom. "Give me a second damn!" Omar shouted as he was caught off guard, lost in his thoughts. After a few moments, he pulled into a parking spot and hopped out. *I need to chill the fuck out... I can't control Ja'Bria and fuck Ja'Bari. He paced towards the front of the line.* "Let me get a three piece and some dirty rice with slaw and iced tea, and tell your homegirl over there not to be rushing customers, damn." He mean mugged the girl for no true reason. "Ummm, okay." The cashier looked at him like he was crazy and fixed his drink. He snatched his food and drink and decided to eat inside. As he chomped down on his chicken dinner he kicked his feet up in the spare chair and scrolled through his social media pages.

Young Boss having a grand opening? Omar snatched his neck back and screenshot the post so he could zoom in on it. "Well what do you know..." A smirk of vengeance spread across his face as he planned to destroy the party in one way or another.

He didn't even tell me he had a studio, much less invite me to the grand opening. Man fuck Young Boss for real. Omar went to young boss' Instagram page and blocked him.

Let me throw this trash away and get fresh for this wack ass party. Step up in there lookin' like a billion dollars. 'Omar who invited you?'. 'I invited myself, why? Who got a problem with it?' Omar rehearsed a mock conversation while pulling up to the mall. After about an hour he was ready to head home. *I'm gon' kill em' with the Bally's.* He smirked as he blasted his homeboys new single and sped through traffic. He pulled into his driveway, grabbed the mail and dashed into the house. *It's been months since I looked at all this mail, let me see what bills I need to catch up on.* He plopped onto the couch as a sudden flashback of Ja'Bria straddling him and softly planting kisses all over his face and lips. A quick feeling of emptiness rushed his body before he tried to regain his thoughts. *What the fuck was I doing? Let me see... Water bill due. Ugh, fashion magazine. Oh yeah, my insurance! Let me sit that on the coffee table. Ja'Bria – confidential? The fuck is this?* Omar's lips went numb and his heart pounded as he slowly opened the tightly sealed- oversized envelope.

Dear Ja'Bria,

This letter is being sent to you in confidence regarding your recent financial activity.

Your financial assets totaling 1.3 million dollars have been secured upon your request and are listed in the attached documents for you records.

If you have any questions regarding your accounts, stocks, bonds, or CD's please don't hesitate to contact us. We are here to serve you every step of the way!

Omar's face felt numb as sweat beads surfaced his nose. He gritted his teeth and threw the papers onto the coffee table. "Sneaky bitch!" he yelled as he snatched off his t-shirt while pacing the floor.

I just need to get back on her good side man I should've married that damn girl, what was I thinking? Omar nearly rubbed the skin off his face as he showered and thought deeply about Ja'Bria and how bad he'd messed up. He dried off, slid into a pair of boxers and crawled into bed for a quick nap. He had worn himself out by overthinking.

Fly Girls

"So what time are y'all going up there?" Tatiana asked Ja'Bria, hardly able to contain herself. "Oh we're on our way out the door. Meet me at the left side parking lot and we can walk in together." "Cool, we' leaving out now too." Tatiana slid into her black Just Cavalli dress. "Hand me that Chanel purse." She pointed at the chase lounge chair as she stepped into her six inch pumps and put on her earrings simultaneously. "Slow down before you break something girl!" Her friend laughed as she handed her the handbag and touched up her lipstick.

"You ever had an eerie feeling but you don't know why?" Ja'Bria asked her homegirl as she turned the music down a few notches. "Yeah why you got a funny feeling about tonight?" "Yeah, I mean I know we're straight but I don't know. Do you need something out of gas station?" She offered as she opened the gas cap. "Some gum and a bottle of water."

"*Hella money, Ganga cash, Ganga cash, hella money, I make it fast bitch I'm bomb hoe!*" The girls sang in unison as they pulled up to the grand opening. "Bambi be killin' it" "she really do." They made small talk while walking to the front door.

"What you doing here with your fine ass?

Smelling and looking like a million." JaBari whispered in Tatiana's ear. Goosebumps covered her neck as she giggled, "move JaBari, I'm still mad at you." Tatiana turned to face him as Ja'Bria walked over. "How in the world were we cooked in the same womb for nine months and I can't get in touch with you to save my life!?" Ja'Bria playfully pushed her brother. Young Boss walked over to introduce himself, "finally I get to meet you, you hide a lot don't you?" he asked jokingly as he moved through the crowd. Ja'Bria nodded and smiled, "hey Young Boss" she replied as if she had known him for years. The music was blasting at a tasteful volume, the atmosphere was perfect and many top celebrities stopped by to congratulate Young Boss.

The fuck is he doing here? Young Boss whispered to himself in disbelief. He pulled out his phone and messaged Ja'Bari *"aye who told O about the grand opening?"* *"You the man, word gets around to the wanna be's too."* Ja'Bari texted as he chuckled to himself. "Seriously Bari, I've been trying to have an important conversation with you for months. What have you been so busy doing? I've looked at real estate property, commercial property and I've been working on a strategic business plan. Out of all people, I expected you to be easier to reach. But enough about me, I got something that's going to change your life." Ja'Bari finally tuned into what his sister was saying. "I hear you, it sounds serious." He raised his eyebrow. "Oh, as a matter of fact, ask YB if we can be the first to grace his conference room. I need to go to the car. I'm almost sure my briefcase with the paperwork is in my trunk." Ja'Bria strutted away as Ja'Bari looked at his sister for a split second in admiration. *Lil sis is bossy on the low, I know she thinks I didn't hear her but I did. I know she's going to be successful. I got a feeling I know what she's been trying to link up about...*

"Boss, let me use your conference room for a minute or two. My sister wants to chop it up about some business." Ja'Bari found Young Boss in the mix mingling. "Of course, set the code on the door if you want to lock it. You can change the code every time. Just press hashtag, hashtag, hashtag." Young Boss answered. "Hashtag!? You mean pound, pound, pound?" They both laughed hysterically as they realized the age difference. Omar scanned the crowd as his eyes landed on Ja'Bari and Young Boss laughing, he instantly felt like they were laughing and talking shit about him. He stormed outside where he spotted Ja'Bria walking away from a handsome dude, "I'm for real, call me, I wanna take you to dinner tomorrow." The guy shouted as he and Ja'Bria parted ways. She yelled okay and walked towards her car. Omar's heart was racing, and his blood was boiling. A few of Tatiana's friends arrived late, they recognized him as they walked towards the door. "Ugh what's wrong with him?" One of the girls said, "girl don't say nothing to him, he looks deranged" they shared a chuckle before walking into the studio.

Ja'Bria unlocked her car door, opened the passenger side door and unlocked the glove compartment. "Oh so you can't answer my calls or nothing" Omar startled her as he shoved her head forward causing her to hit her forehead on the dashboard. "Oh my gosh! Get the fuck off me!" She screamed nearly losing her voice. She thrust all of her dead weight backwards, violently pushing him off her as she slammed the glove compartment shut. Enraged, she charged towards him and chocked him with all her might. "So you just come up on some money and leave me bitch!?" Omar spat with venom on his tongue. "After all I've done for you? Oh yeah and yo brother knows you a snake too, dirty bitch" he continued as he lunged in to choke her. "Fuck you, I don't owe you shit!" She barked swiftly and moved away from him. The vacant tour bus that was parked horizontally in front of her car quickly became her shelter, she slipped around it and sprinted right out of her Dior pumps. Omar became irate and irrational all at once. He pulled out his 9mm as Ja'Bria tripped and scraped the side of her leg. "Ouuuch" Pop! Omar's thumb hand caused his gun to let off a single shot to Ja'Bria's face. "Oh my God! What did I do?" He whispered as he ran. He kept his eyes on Ja'Bria's bloody face for as long as he could.

"They shootin'!" A bystander shouted. "Hell yeah, run!" Omar added as he thought quick on his feet. He hopped in his car and sped off before many people could see him.

"Ja'Bari somebody said your sister was shot just now, hurry up!" Tatiana frantically cried as she stood at the door to the conference room. "My sister!? By who!? What!?" He leaped from the conference table to the door and snatched it open. "Where the fuck is my sister?" He snatched the door opened and bullied his way through the gossiping crowd repeating himself. Nobody had the answers, he raced through the crowd eyeing every female that resembled Ja'Bria in any way. Once he made it to the door, he saw an ambulance pulling off and Police Officers taping an area off. "Sir you can't go down there." An officer grabbed Ja'Bari's arm. "Fuck you" Ja'Bari spat back as he swiftly walked towards the yellow crime scene tape. "Where is my twin sister?" He demanded answers. "Sir we have no evidence of a body, just a small puddle of blood and this bullet shell." Detective Louis responded as he held up a plastic bag with a fresh bullet shell in it. "Here's my card, keep in touch." "Nooooo, man fuck!" Ja'Bari cried as he punched the side of the tour bus. He slowly walked around searching for some sign of Ja'Bria but there was nothing. "God please, whatever you do, don't take my sister from me. She's all I have God, please, God please, God please." He cried as he banged his head on the steering wheel. "Baby, there you are. What happened?" Tatiana said as she raced to the driver's seat to comfort Ja'Bari. "I don't know." He whimpered as he took a deep breath and cried on his girlfriend's chest. "I don't even see her car, what the hell is really going on?" Tatiana was puzzled. "Get in the passenger seat bae, let's go to the hospital." Tatiana pulled him by his arms. Her mind raced as she fixed the rearview mirror and buckled her seatbelt. "I got a feeling she's okay." Ja'Bari broke the silence. "I do too…". Tatiana calmly replied as she pulled into the ER parking garage. *Click clack, click clack*, Tatiana's six inch pumps echoed throughout the parking garage as her heart raced. Ja'Bari wasn't far behind her as he checked their surroundings, he knew something was fishy and he wasn't going to rest until he got to the bottom of it all. Flashbacks of his and Omar's conversation resurfaced in his mind as he rubbed his chin, his gut assured him Omar had everything to do with whatever was going on. "Ja'Bria Browns room please, I'm her twin brother, next of kin, here's my ID." Ja'Bari's sweaty hands began to shake. "The receptionist took his ID and searched for a Ja'Bria Brown but she found nothing. "I'm sorry sir, there is no J Brown in this hospital, I've searched on every list there is." "She has to be here." He dryly objected. "Nope, she's not here." The receptions confirmed as she logged out of the computer and walked away.

"Arghhhhh!" Ja'Bari punched the desk out of frustration and walked towards the large bay windows to the left of the main entrance. "Baby calm down. That means she's okay, right?", Tatiana calmly hugged him. *"Dear Lord, wrap your arms around Ja'Bria and protect her. Keep her safe in your arms Lord and keep Ja'Bari in good spirits. Show him that his sister is okay. Give him the same favor that you gave him when you allowed him to share his mother's womb with her Lord. Give him the twin intuition that he needs to be comforted. In your name we pray. – Amen"*. Tatiana prayed as warm tears streamed down Ja'Bari's face. "I don't have a ring right now or anything but will you marry me?" He asked as he kneeled down on one knee and gently kissed Tatiana's left hand. "Yes, yes, I'll marry you." Tatiana shook her head as tears dropped onto Ja'Bari's forehead. There they were in the main entrance of the quiet and empty hospital praying and holding one another.

Three Days Missing

"Hi Detective, any word about the incident at the studio? We still haven't spoken to Ja'Bria." Tatiana said into the phone as she gazed down at her two karat ring. "We' issued a silver alert. I'm not sure what else you want me to do," he responded as he gulped down a mug of coffee. *CLICK* – Tatiana slammed the phone down so hard that the ink pen and notebook flew off the night stand. Tears rolled down her face as she slid off the edge of the bed and walked into the bathroom. Her mind raced as she mumbled to herself, *I know she's okay, she has to be....* Although Ja'Bari was the last person to see Ja'Bria reportedly alive, Tatiana somehow kept subconsciously blaming herself. Desperate for answers, Tatiana called Omar. "Where is she!? What did you do to Ja'Bria!?" With sweaty palms and numb lips his heart raced as he answered. "What are you talking about? What did you do to her?" he responded as his left knee jumped out of control. He stepped on the gas pedal and continued to race down the highway with no clear direction. "Why would I even answer the phone if I shot her?" He screamed into the receiver without thinking. "You what!?" she screamed right before he hung up. As her mind raced, Tatiana quickly went to her last iMessages from Omar and tapped the information option, and sure enough his current location was there. *Stupid ass didn't even stop sharing his location! Snap!* She screen shot the map of his location and sent it to Ja'Bari. "He just admitted that he shot Ja'Bria!" She screamed into the receiver before Ja'Bari could answer. "Slow down baby, what are you talking about?" Ja'Bari swerved into the driveway of a new property he was about to show. "Where are you?" She frantically asked. "I'm working Tatiana, what the hell is going on!?" Tatiana immediately began explaining that she called Omar and asked what he did to Ja' because he was a prime suspect in her eyes. She then told him that Omar blurted out that he didn't shoot Ja'Bria but she never said anything about shooting. "Baby calm down, maybe you accidentally said something about a shooting. Surely his punk ass wouldn't have the guts to do something like that." He assured himself and Tatiana as he drifted into a flashback of when Omar came to him about Ja'Bria being shady and withholding information from them. "Let me call you back, I'll be home in a little bit." He hung up and called his clients to ask where they were. "We got lost, we're pulling into the community now" the lady cheerfully answered. Ja'Bari thanked the lady and hung up as he paced back and forth across the marble floors. He focused on clearing his mind as his clients pulled into the round driveway.

"It's beautiful, what do you think honey?" The lady asked her husband as they admired and inspected the home. "It's amazing, I actually like it better than the other one. Let's take a look upstairs." The husband suggested as Ja'Bari opted to stay downstairs and allow them to explore. *Sis, if you can see this, answer me. I love you and I got your back through anything. Let me know what you need, we had a meeting we never made. Please text me back.* Ja'Bari texted Ja'Bria hoping she would respond. He stared at his phone to see if the message was delivered but after he didn't see any results two or three minutes later, he closed his messages out and surfed Instagram. He searched Omar's Instagram name. *He deleted his account? He is definitely up to something, all he cared about was having over 10k followers, he got it and deleted his account? Oh hell nah...* Ja'Bari thought to himself as he looked at his text messages. *New York!? Boerum Hill District is in New York. Bond Street, Pacific Street, yeah he's definitely in New York. I got something for his ass.* Ja'Bari snapped out of it and realized he was at work. It had been thirty minutes, "How is everything up there?" He asked as he jogged up the steps. Caught off guard, the male client quickly slipped out of the master bedroom and placed his arm around Ja'Bari's neck in a chokehold position. "Don't think it's a game, you gotta be quicker than that." "What the fu.." "Shut up! Bae..." The man shouted as the lady stepped out of the bedroom from across the hall with a chrome 22 millimeter pistol pointed directly at Ja'Bari's forehead. "Try anything funny and it's over." The man released Ja'Bari and shoved him towards the spiral staircase. Ja'Bari took a few steps forward and turned around to walk backwards down the steps. "If you shoot me, I'll be looking you in the eyes." He scowled as he slowly walked backwards. As he got halfway down the steps the front door swung open. "Be smart Ja'Bari, where's the cash?" Karla coldly said. He swung around in disbelief, "you too? What the fuck?" "Shut up. You could've been paying me more this whole time, yeah Omar told me…" She started before she was cut off by the client, "KK shut up and stick to the script." The man demanded as Ja'Bari's feet hit the floor. "What's this all about? Come on man, don't shoot a real one. You need to be aiming…" "Shut the fuck up before I pop you right here, right now!" The lady yelled as she cocked the gun, she was the last one to enter the open foyer. Ja'Bari stood there ready to lose his life, he had three guns pointed at his dome, a missing twin sister and a disloyal worker. "I ain't got shit, shoot me, I don't even give a fuck no more!" He shouted fearlessly as he beat on his chest with his fists. "Shoot me motherfuckers, shoot me!" He screamed finally breaking down crying. "Get yo punk ass up, don't nobody want to kill you. Where's the money?" The man yelled as he kicked Ja'Bari with the gun still pointed at him. Both the man and woman client were focused on Ja'Bari when Karla quickly cocked her gun and shot them twice. "Ja'Bari get up, I didn't come here to kill you, I came here to save you, I'm in love with you" she said as she kneeled down and kissed him endlessly. She attempted to climb on top of him as blood quickly oozed out of the lifeless bodies. Ja'Bari kicked the gun across the marble floor as he jumped up. "Get off of me you crazy bitch!" He ran quickly towards the door as she screamed and cried, "I killed for you! I would die for you. I love you Ja'Bari! Come back!" She pleaded as she cried and looked back at the blood bath. Ja'Bari jumped into his car, placed it in reverse and rammed Karla's car out of the driveway and into the woods. He put the car in drive and sped off full speed. "What the fuck!?" He screamed as he called Tatiana. "Pack everything that's important to you. Hurry up. Get everything out of the safe, the code is 122310. Oh, and pack some of my sweat suits and Nikes. Hurry up!" He said as he sped home on the back streets. His mind raced as he contemplated calling Young Boss. *Is he behind this shit too!? What the fuck, I swear to God I am going to kill Omar if it's the last thing I ever fucking do!* He promised himself as he zipped into the driveway and scanned his surroundings. "Baby why do you have blood on your shirt, what is going on?" Tatiana cried as she shoved the last few items into the oversized suitcase. Ja'Bari ignored her as he snatched his clothes off and jumped into the shower. Her mind raced as she frantically searched each room for things they might need. Ja'Bari stepped out of the shower, wrapped a towel around his hips and threw his clothes in a trash bag. "Are you okay?" She asked as she caressed his face. "Yeah bae, I'm good. I'll tell you everything when we get in the car." He said as he looked around the room. He grabbed a pair of grey sweats and a white tee that wasn't packed. After getting dressed, he slipped on a pair of white socks and Nike flip-flops and grabbed his pistol off the dresser. Tatiana went back downstairs to drag the last suitcase into the garage. "I hope we're taking the Infiniti truck, that's where the luggage is," she yelled upstairs. "Yep." Ja'Bari answered. He made his final check around the house as his mind raced. "The mail, let me check the mail. Grab the keys, meet me outside," he directed as he closed the front door behind himself. Tatiana cranked the SUV and opened the garage door. *Zoom, zoom, zoom...* Three motorcycles zipped past the house as Ja'Bari opened the mailbox. His heart dropped and he automatically grabbed his pistol and turned to face the bikers, once he saw them making a U-turn at the cul-de-sac, he kept his eyes on them until they were out of sight. Anxiety filled his body from head to toe as he grabbed the overflowing mail and hopped into the passenger seat. "Where are we going?" Tatiana asked as she watched the garage door close. "Just hit the highway, we'll figure it out in a minute." He started telling her about Karla and the whole set up at the house he was showing. "What the fuck!? Does Young Boss know about this or did he have something to do with it too? What is going on Ja'Bari and where the hell is Ja'Bria because she isn't dead, she can't be. You would have gotten a phone call by now, you're her next of kin. Right? She's not dead, right?" Tatiana was trying to convince herself while tears streamed down her face. "Bae, if you can't drive without being all emotional and shit, pull over and let me drive." He gritted through his teeth as he tried not to raise his voice. She took a deep breath and didn't respond, she just listened as he continued telling her how he met the clients and everything. "They found me online for a house that I have listed as the agent. Omar is playing a dirty game and people are getting killed behind it. We gotta do something quick. The location you screenshot and sent me is in New York. I have no idea what he's doing up there but I wonder if we should go and I should just finish his ass before he does anything else or if I should lay low for a few days and come up with a solid plan." He babbled as Tatiana got into the fast lane. "Bari, whatever you want to do, you need to figure it out quick." She exclaimed as she sped up. "Slow down!" He shouted as he looked in the rearview mirror. "I just told you what happened, I don't need no cops stopping us or nothing right now, I don't even know what's going to happen at that house but my name is all over the listing and I'm documented as showing it to the two people that are laying in the floor dead right now man, fuck!" He hit the glove compartment. "Okay, we're going to the beach. You need some peace and quiet. We're going to Hilton Head where it's quiet and low key." She said as she side eyed him. He didn't say anything he just took a deep breath and thanked God for her.

Check In

"Three nights to start with, here's my ID." Tatiana slapped her cousin's driver's license on the counter and dug in her handbag so she didn't have to look the reservation agent in the eyes, luckily they accepted cash deposits. Ja'Bari sat in the car and scoped out the parking lot, his idle mind began to wonder if she was trying to set him up too. He checked his clip on his pistol and prayed for the best. *God please let her have my back, my back is against the wall and I don't have a soul I trust right now. Make her trustworthy, make sure she's whole and pure. If she isn't show me immediately so I can get away from her too. – Amen*

"Got us a complimentary upgrade to the highest floor and we got a suite for the price of a deluxe room, ocean view and all!" She bragged as she hopped back into the car. "That's what's up. I hope it's not all the way at the top to make it hard for me to escape from more fuckery." He sucked his teeth and rolled his eyes. "Man chill out, nobody knows where we are. You got the GPS disabled on this car before you brought it home remember?" She assured him. "Yeah…" He nodded, knowing he couldn't fully trust himself much less her. She parked on the fifth floor of the parking deck and popped the trunk.

"Grab your duffle bag, I have a few changes of clothes in there for us." She said as she grabbed her overnight bag and stuffed the mail in it. They walked towards the elevators, the hotel wasn't busy at all. "It's really quiet around here, a little too quiet if you ask me," Ja'Bari said. "That's a good thing right?" Tatiana asked as she rolled her eyes and breathed through her nose, *I'm doing everything I can and he still can't at least say thank you? Ugh...* She thought to herself as they approached the 22nd floor.

They both sat quietly for a few moments while they collected their thoughts. "Give me the mail." Ja'Bari said breaking the ice. "Oh here you go." Tatiana pulled out two piles of mail. He flipped through the junk mail throwing it in the trash until he got to a thick blue envelope that looked like a birthday card. He pulled the card out of the envelope and opened it, ten cashier's checks fell out of the card and it read *Congrats on your wedding engagement!* Ja'Bari looked puzzled as he slowly read each check written to him for the same amount of $100,000. "Who is it from?" Tatiana asked as she gasped. "There's no name, there's no return address, there's no signature, there's no handwriting on this..." He stopped in mid-sentence as he tried to make out the signature on the bottom of the checks. "The name starts with a 'B' but I can't tell what it says." "Who did you tell that we were getting married?" He asked as he studied each cashier's check over and over.

"Nobody, I haven't had a chance to talk to anybody, everything has happened so fast, who did you tell?" "Same here, nobody." He responded as he stacked the checks and placed them back into the envelope and sat it off to the side. "Is this some sort of sick joke or is it really a million dollars' worth of certified checks sitting on the bed?" Ja'Bari asked as he cocked his head to the side and shuffled through the rest of the mail. After pondering on whether the mail was a cruel joke or a real check, Ja'Bari went on the balcony to blaze and clear his mind. "Bae, order room service. I want a steak or something…" He stared at the sunset and let the ocean waves soothe his nerves. He decided to face his fears and make a few phone calls the next day before things got worse. *We're going back home after this mini vacation. Ain't nobody running me out of my own town. I run that shit, can't nobody take it away from me. From now on, I'll just move a little different. Switch up a few things and replace a few people. It is what it is, life goes on. Maybe it was just a fluke at the house showing the other day. The certified checks probably are real… Blessed…* Ja'Bari inhaled the fresh sea salty air and exhaled as he smiled.

Giving Face

"Briana, Briana, it's me, Doctor McKinnie. Your surgery is over. Blink if you can hear me." The bright lights shined directly on her face "ughhh". The doctors turned the bright lights off and slowly raised the bed as they handed her pamphlets. "Your face mask can come off in two days, your cheek lift isn't major but you will notice a difference. Leave the cast on your nose for at least seven days, we recommend ten days. Your eye lift has slightly changed the shape and appearance of your eyes. We suggest you take it easy for the next seven days and avoid any medicines that enhance bleeding such as aspirin, ibuprofen, vitamin E and even herbal teas for at least two weeks if possible." Doctor McKinnie advised Briana. Her lips were numb so she couldn't respond, she merely shot the doctor a thumbs up and looked around the room. "You can stay in here for another hour or longer if you need to and if you'd prefer someone drive you home, feel free to leave your car here. We have exclusive car service providers or you can call a taxi, it's up to you. The doctor continued. Briana lifted her head and waved her hands in a declining motion.

Three hours later Briana pulled into the garage of her new condo in Santa Monica, CA. She slowly walked inside and felt a sense of relief. *It doesn't look bad from what I can see. I hope I look beautiful when I take off these masks and casts.* She giggled to herself as she cracked open her laptop and began searching for the best bleaching creams and soaps for her skin. *I don't really want to bleach my skin but I probably should. I wonder what will make me just one shade lighter? Maybe I should try a light version, maybe they have different strengths, that would be good.* She smiled through her sore face and looked around at her living room, everything in the condo was white with mirrored or glass furniture. *Ahhh, it feels good to be in a new place on the beach with beautiful views and friendly neighbors.*

Ding-Dong, knock-knock-knock. Briana nearly jumped out of her skin as she tip-toed towards the front door and looked through the peep hole. She could see a delivery person but she didn't trust it so she stood there perfectly silent until he left a vase on the front door steps and drove off. She quickly opened the door and looked around, everything looked normal. She grabbed the vase and slammed the door shut making sure to latch every lock. She carried the oversized vase with 48 beautiful roses back into the living room and read the note. She gasped loudly and dropped the vase as it shattered into a million pieces.

THE CONCEALED TRUTH

MANDI MAC

Coming Soon!

Fountain Pen Publishing LLC